My Turn to Dump You

Guerline Fenelon Jean Pierre

Table of Contents

My Turn to Dump You i

Guerline Fenelon Jean Pierre i

Copyright © 2019 by Guerline Fenelon Jean Pierre. ii

All Rights Reserved. ii

ISBN: 978-0-578-59495-8 ii

Chapter 1 1

Chapter 2 8

Chapter 3 14

Chapter 4 19

Chapter 5 27

Chapter 6 35

Chapter 7 42

Chapter 8 48

Chapter 9 55

Chapter 10 62

Chapter 11 67

Chapter 12 74

Chapter 13 81

Chapter 14 90

Chapter 15 97

Chapter 16 106

Chapter 17 113

Chapter 18 120

Chapter 19...132

Chapter 20...141

Chapter 21...147

Chapter 22...154

Chapter 23...161

Chapter 24...165

Chapter 1

Dina started dating Derrick since her first year at the Colossal University in Baltimore, Maryland. For the first time in her life she was away from home, away from her family, and could finally do whatever she wanted. Derrick was a senior in Medical, while Dina was a freshman in Law. But it wasn't the only difference between them; Dina was an introvert tall black girl, while Derrick was an outgoing white boy. They were mostly together, and all their friends at the campus knew about their relationship.

They moved in with each other, and Derrick told Dina that he wanted to marry her as soon as he graduates. So, later, when Dina heard a rumor about Derrick and another female student at the campus, she did not believe it. However, at the insistence of one of her best friends, Miranda, Dina decided to discuss the matter with Derrick. He denied the allegation, but Dina found him so edgy that she suspected he did not tell her the truth; therefore, she started to spy on him.

A few weeks later Dina had evidence of what she feared the most: Derrick was cheating on her. She found him arm in arm with a brunette, at the snack bar of the movie theater, just two miles away from their campus. This time, Dina confronted him, and he admitted that he was dating the brunette as well.

Not able to deal with the betrayal of her boyfriend, Dina decided to leave the campus and returned to her parent's house.

"Call me anytime if you need to talk." Said Miranda

"I will," answered Dina.

"You know what, I still believe it is not a good decision to abandon your study because of Derrick. He is graduating in just a few months; you should stay and continue your study" declared Miranda

"I know, but I am not leaving specifically because of him; I also need a little distance away from all of this, to think and find myself; I feel so lost you know" explained Dina

"I understand. I just wish that I could do something..." Expressed Miranda.

"I know, but I need to go through this alone. You should hurry now; your classes will begin soon." Replied Dina

Miranda grabbed her binders and her calculator and placed them in her backpack; she went to Dina and hugged her, then, she walked towards the entrance door and opened it...

"You take care of yourself, okay." Said Miranda

"You too," replied Dina

Miranda closed the door behind her and went to class as fast as she could.

After Miranda left, Dina started to prepare her baggage. While gathering her belongings, she found one of the pictures that she took with Derrick, in which Derrick was holding her in his arms and she was laying her head on his chest. Dina remember the day that she and Derrick took this picture, they were coming from the ice cream parlor near their campus when Derrick asked one of his fellow classmates to take the photo for him and Dina.

Dina and Derrick loved the picture so much that they decided to print it. A few days later, Derrick brought a romantic picture frame with a frosted glass and mounted the picture into it. "He seemed to be happy with me, I really didn't see that coming," said Dina to herself.

Something came in her mind like a poem to express her regret:

"Why did I have to spy on you?
I should have ignore your infidelity
We used to be in the same crew
But now you and I are history."
"Why did you cheat on me
You could have just admitted
That you were seeing her
Now that from me you're free
I feel so defeated
To be the sole loser"
"One day or another
You will feel my furor
I know I will recover

And fall in love once more."

Dina placed the glass picture frame between two shirts in her luggage to keep the frame from breaking and proceeded to close the suitcase. "Maybe I should give him a call, I'm sure that, by now, he must regret dating that girl on my back; he might even have already dump her. Perhaps once I get back home, he will call me to know how I'm doing, and to tell me how sorry he is. If only I had stoped spying on him, I would still be with the love of my life..." thought Dina

After Dina finished to prepare her bags, she called a taxi to drop her to the intercity bus station. From the station, she took the bus, and went to her parents' house in Olney, Maryland. There, she enrolled in a medical assisting program at the county community college and graduated two years later with an associate degree in medical assisting.

Dina was so happy, now that she had a profession, she could secure a job and realize her dreams: move into her own apartment and buy a car. So far, she must borrow her parents' car, or get a ride from one of them when she has an appointment. "But first," thought Dina, "I must find a job."

A song of thanksgiving came to her mind to think Jesus the Lord for allowing her to earn her associate's degree.

"Thank You Lord Jesus,
You are our Savior
With You guiding us
We are always victor."
"You are Alpha and Omega
The Grand Jehovah
You created the universe
And make us so diverse"
"Every day of our life
You watch over us
And when we are in strife
In You we place our trust"
"You bless whoever search
For Your grace and favor
For You created the earth
To give You praise and honor."

Dina bowed on her knees and prayed to God; then, she sat at her computer and began to search for medical assistant jobs on the internet. She replied to a few job postings that were not far from her parents' house.

Two weeks later, Dina received an e-mail from a Doctor's office, informing her that she had an interview the next morning, at 9 a.m. She was happy and anxious at the same time: "what should I wear? Would I be able to answer the questions properly? Would I get the job?" Dina had all these questions bubbling up in her head.

First, Dina decided to go into her closet to choose what she wanted to wear. There were not a lot of clothes to choose from, since she did not go to shop for almost two years. Since her parents had spent most of their savings on her education when they sent her to that expensive law school, they could no longer afford to buy new clothes even for themselves.

Dina opted for a blue, short sleeve dress with a back-zip closure and crew neckline, "this one is perfect," she thought, "it is neither too long nor too short, and I feel very comfortable in it." Then she went online to do a little research on the Doctor's office where she had the interview. Unfortunately, all she could found was the kind of services they provided and their address, which was already in the e-mail that they sent to her. She wished that she could learn something about her potential employer, but it only stipulated that the office was under a new management.

"Well," said Dina to herself, "just try your best; be confident and you'll see."

While she was on the internet, she decided to log in her social page to contact Miranda and see if Derrick did not send her any message yet. Dina was disappointed when she discovered that none of the messages that she had were from Derrick.

While scrolling down on her social page, Dina saw that her friend Miranda had posted some new pictures, she liked every picture, and then, tried to communicate with Miranda via online chat, but unfortunately, Miranda was offline.

Dina was about to click on Derrick's profile to unfriend him when she heard a noise… someone was knocking at her bedroom door…

After the third loud knocks on her door, Dina went and opened it, thinking that it was her brother, Ted, coming to spy on her as usual. Instead, it was Julie, their neighbor's daughter who was standing in front of her.

"Hi, Dina," said Julie.

"Hey, Julie, what a surprise!" replied Dina ironically.

Dina wasn't really surprised, because Julie often came to her house, even too often... Their parents were longtime neighbors and friends; so, when Julie wanted to go somewhere, she knew that if she invited Dina, she had a better chance that her parents would let her go. Julie was twenty-two and Dina was only two years older than her. Julie's parents appreciated Dina because she didn't like to hang out late at night with friends, and they often cited her to Julie as an example to follow.

"Looks like I'm interrupting" said Julie.

Dina felt guilty seeing Julie looking so sad suddenly.

"Alright," said Dina, "I already finish what I was doing. What can I do for you?" Said Dina

"I just came by to ask you if you want to accompany us at the Antilleans night club tonight." Replied Julie

"Did you say *us*?" Asked Dina.

"Yeah, Lucas and I." Replied Julie.

"Let me guess: your parents told you that you are not going, unless I come along with you, right?" asked Dina

"Yeah, but..." started Julie

"Sorry Julie, I really don't have time to play chaperone tonight," declared Dina. Being brought up in a Christian home, Dina never felt comfortable in this kind of place.

"Fine," replied Julie. "Anyway, it's already five o'clock, my birthday has almost past." She added.

"Oh! today is your birthday? how did I forget that! Okay, sit right here," said Dina, while patting her bed to show Julie where to sit. Once Julie sat in the bed, Dina added: "tell me everything now, in case your parents asked. You can just tell them that I'm going with you." Explained Dina

"No!" Exclaimed Julie

"No? why not?" Asked Dina. "It is not like you never did that before. Besides, this is the only way for you to go to this night club with your boyfriend tonight, as I must go to bed early. Now, tell me about every place that you guys planned to go, at what time will you be there, and around what time you will you be back."

"No," repeated firmly Julie, "this time I do not want you to just tell them that I'm with you."

"But why?" asked Dina, "did your parents have any suspicion?" enquired Dina

"No" answer Julie, "I just really want you to come with us tonight."

"Look, I am really sorry Julie, but I have a very important appointment tomorrow morning." Said Dina

"Yep, I understand," said sadly Julie while standing, "it's more important than my birthday...I'll leave then."

"Wait Julie," replied Dina, "it is a job interview that I have tomorrow, I must go to bed early tonight. Why don't you check with Ted? I'm sure he will be happy to escort you." Proposed Dina

"I already did," explained Julie, "Ted said that he has an engagement tonight. But Dina, if you really want to, you can come with us; I promise you, we will back before ten o'clock," assured Julie.

"I don't know..." said Dina, undecided.

"Say yes please," begged Julie. "Besides, you seem stressed out about this interview; having fun and dancing tonight will help you a lot tomorrow, trust me."

"I think that you are right," replied Dina, convinced.

"Perfect!" Exclaimed Julie; "I will pick you up tonight at seven then."

"Okay," replied Dina, "see you in two hours."

After Julie had left, Dina opened her piggy bank box and took twenty dollars from it and put it in her purse to pay for her drink at the club. Then, she went to her parents in the living room. They were watching the news.

"Mom, Dad, I'm going out with Julie tonight." Announced Dina

"Where?" Asked her mother

"At the Antilleans nightclub," said Dina.

"Well it's been a long time since you went out, enjoy your night," replied her mother.

Dina's father wasn't happy about her daughter hanging out at night with Julie. "You know this girl is trouble, you do not have to please her every time and do whatever she asks you to, Dina. You know better." He said with his Haitian accent.

"I know dad, but today is her birthday, I couldn't refuse," explained Dina

"Okay," said her father, "I understand but, do me a favor: after tonight, try to be less available for her so she can work things out with her parents. You're not helping them at all. They want what is best for Julie. It cannot be that hard for you to tell her *no*, your brother just did; I wonder why you always must please her. I heard that some of her friends are not very recommendable.

"It's just her boyfriend and her who are going," replied Dina.

"Good, but remember, her parents trust you and expect that you would help her being better, not the opposite," said her father.

"Ok, dad I promise I will start telling her no after tonight." replied Dina

"Thanks, I know you would understand," added her father.

He took his wallet from his pocket, removed a fifty dollars bill from it, and handled it to Dina.

"Here to pay for your drink." said her father

"Oh, I already took a twenty-dollar bill from my piggy bank dad," replied Dina

"Take it just in case, you never know," advised her father, "and have a safe night." He added.

"Thanks dad," said Dina, while taking the money. After that, Dina went to the kitchen, opened the refrigerator, and took a yogurt. She opened one of the silverware drawers, grabbed a spoon, closed the drawer and went back to her room. She took her purse and added the fifty dollars bill to the twenty.

Once again, Dina sat in front of her computer; as she was already logged in her social page, she clicked the friends' button, and her friends list immediately appeared. Dina selected Derrick's profile and unfriended him. "Almost two years, and you never contacted me. It's the only way for me to forget about you Derrick," thought Dina. A poem of resignation came to her mind:

"I know I'm still in love with you
But since you don't want me anymore
I have decided to forget you too
Maybe one day you will knock at my door."
"You are a cheater, and a liar
I thought you were the one
But you are just a con
You made me step closer, to the line of fire
I'm glad that you had fun
Now my game is on."
"I believed that you and I
Were together forever
But your betrayal
Had caused us to scatter."

Then, Dina logged out of her social page, and started eating her yogurt.

Chapter 2

While scooping out her yogurt with the spoon, Dina was thinking about the conversation that she just had with her father regarding Julie. "Julie is not that bad," thought Dina, "she is just a typical girl of her time who likes partying late at night, and sometimes needs guidance." But Dina's parents were born and raised in Haiti, and consequently believed that girls should stay home at night, not hanging out with friends in nightclubs.

Dina and her brother Ted were also born in Haiti, but their parents immigrated with them in the United States when Dina was four years old and Ted was just two. Her family never went back to Haiti, even for vacation. Their parents said that it was too dangerous; they heard that the insecurity was affecting the Haitian diaspora visiting the country more than foreigners. Native Haitians are more targeted when they go there to visit because they are perceived as people who come with money to distribute to family members and friends, or to buy land or houses.

However, Dina and her brother knew as much Haitian words and foods as any other person raised in Haiti. They spoke Kreyol fluently, and Dina, particularly, as the only girl in the family, knew how to cook most of Haitian dishes like ground corn with vegetables called "mayi moulen ak legim" in Kreyol, white rice with black or white beans which is "diri kole ak pwa," rice with black mushroom and green peas called "diri ak djondjon;" not to mention "griot" and "taso" with plantains, one of her favorite food that Haitian people called fritay.

As for her brother Ted, he visited the kitchen only to taste the food and know how it's supposed to look when it is well done in case that his wife is not a good cooker as she should. Their mother also taught to Dina how to wash her future husband's clothes, as it is presumed that Ted's wife will be responsible to do his laundry.

Dina tried to explain to her parents that this kind of education was outdated, and will not benefit Ted, and that nowadays, both men and women must learn to do housework chores such as cooking, cleaning, laundering and grocery shopping as well. However, her parents never took her advice.

Dina endured all this sexism at home, and from time to time, showed some resistance by trying to address her family tradition that caused her to be subject to all this inequity, but like most Haitian descent girls, she did the household chores to make life easier on her folks.

In addition, her family was still attached to Haiti's custom and culture; every January 1st, which is the Haitian Independence Day, her mother always cooks pumpkin soup, a dish made of pumpkin and all kind of vegetables plus goat, and beef meats that Haitian people proudly call "soup joumou."

Dina thought of how much her family was different from their neighbors' family; Julie and her parents were all born and raised in the States. This explains why Julie is so autonomous. In addition, Julie does not like too many rules, but prefers to do what she wants to do, not what her parents expect from her. Unlike Dina, Julie did not have any cultural barriers or any kind of curfew. She grew up in a modern and liberal family.

At 7:00 p.m. precisely, Julie and her boyfriend picked up Dina in front of her house and drove straight to the Antilleans nightclub. There were so many people; they found a table near the bar. Julie's boyfriend, Lucas, asked her and Dina what they wanted to drink.

"I will take a Martini," said Julie.

"A soda please," said Dina to Lucas, who was waiting for her to decide.

Julie and Lucas looked at each other and laughed.

"What!?" asked Dina, surprised

"Nothing," replied Julie. "I was thinking that maybe you should take something stronger than a soda to relax. You should see how tense you appeared to be."

Dina thought a moment and conceded:

"Okay, I will take a Martini too."

"Well, that's better," said Lucas "I am going to order them now."

Dina opened her purse and hand over the fifty dollars bill that her father gave her to Lucas. "Here's the money for my drink," said Dina

"Keep your money for now," replied Lucas, "I'm going to open a tab, so we won't have to pay each time we order, and we will divide the bill three ways, and pay for everything before we leave."

"Okay," agreed Dina; she put the money back in her purse, and Lucas left to buy the drinks.

"Thank you for coming, said Julie to Dina. We're really going to have fun tonight."

"Please do not thank me" said Dina; "I think that I really need to chill out a little bit and have some fun tonight as you said. Oh, I almost forgot, "happy birthday," shouted Dina to Julie while handling a pink bag to her.

"A present for me," exclaimed Julie, who rapidly opened the bag

"Aw, it's a beautiful scarf; thanks, Dina," exclaimed Julie

The scarf was one of the many presents that Derrick gave Dina. It still had the tag on, for she had never used it. It was also one of the few gifts that she kept and didn't give to Miranda when she was leaving the university to come home.

Lucas returned with the drinks, sat down and started a lively conversation with Dina and Julie. He even explained to Dina how grateful he was to her for accepting to come with them, which allow Julie to be able to be with him.

Julie and Lucas were laughing and drinking as they conversed, they were having fun. "Lucas and Julie looked so cute together" thought Dina, who always perceived Julie just as an intrusive person, and not this cheery girl.

After a while, Dina who was not really engaged in their conversation become bored. Even though the place was full of people, she felt isolated and started staring at the table to distract herself from the awkwardness of the situation.

To relieve her discomfort, Dina picked up the glass of martini, and drank all her beverage at once. Julie who was observing her also drank the rest of her martini, and asked Lucas to go order a second drink for them.

"I think it is going to be my last drink, I am not going to get another one after that, so you can take my money to pay for mine now." Proposed Dina

"Oh yeah," agreed Lucas, "it will be the last ones for Julie and me too." He added while taking the money from Dina.

Lucas came back with the drinks, placed one in front of Julie and passed the other one to Dina. "Here's your change," said Lucas to Dina while handling her the loose change. As soon as he handed the drink to Julie, she took the garnish olive pick and mixed it to her beverage before placing the glass between her lips and drank the whole glass.

Right away, Lucas got up, took Julie's hand and led her to the dance floor.

Dina sat alone. She looked at them dancing and felt a twinge for the first time in a while. She felt lonely. She remembered how Derrick and her used to go to dance on weekends. A tear rolled down her cheek, she wiped it quickly with the back of her hand, grabbed the glass and drank a sip of her drink. At the same time a gentleman approached her, and asked: "how are you doing tonight?"

"Good," answered Dina, surprised. "What about you?" She asked

The gentleman held out his hand and replied: "I think I might feel better if you would dance with me. Would you?"

Dina looked at him; he was handsome and very well dressed. Without answering, she gave him her right hand, but before getting up, she drank all the rest of her martini, and ate the olive that was used to garnish it, and finally got up to dance with him.

They danced for a while without saying a word to each other. Dina felt so good that she wanted to stay like that indefinitely.

After a moment, the gentleman whispered in her ear:

"My name is Gavin, what's yours?"

There was so much noise that she had to put her mouth close to his ear, so he could hear her.

"Call me whatever you want." whispered Dina

"Well... I will call you Blue, then." Proposed Gavin.

"Blue? Why Blue?" Asked Dina

"Because you are wearing a blue dress." Said Gavin.

Dina laughed, and Gavin smiled. "And he has a good sense of humor too." Thought Dina.

Then, Gavin asked her: "What do you do in life?"

"You mean since he left me?" Replied Dina, nostalgic.

"Oh, ok" exclaimed Gavin, astonished, "If this is what you want to talk about…"

"I left the campus, went back to live with my parents and I miss him SOOO much." Explained Dina

Suddenly, the music stopped, and the DJ started playing a slow jam. Many couples returned to their seats, Dina was about to go back to her table when Gavin grabbed and retained her hand, Dina gripped his hand back, and without saying a word, he drew her close to him.

Instinctively, Dina put her head on his shoulder, and followed his rhythm. "I didn't feel so good like that for so long, thought Dina. She closed her eyes hoping that this moment would last forever…

And in her head a melody was playing, differently from the music that the DJ was performing:

"I feel so good that it sounds

Like I finally found

The guy that is right for me

Maybe it is destiny
I want to stay in his arms
My heart his voice warms."
"I didn't see him coming
I guess he saw my coast was clear
And then I heard his soothing tone
Gentle like a calming song
I want to stay in this loving
And fiery atmosphere
This guy is my partner of choice
For so long I didn't feel that poise"
Suddenly, Dina felt a pat on her back, she turned around and realized it was Julie.

"What?" Asked Dina

"Sorry to interrupt but it is ten o'clock, we must go." Said Julie

"Oh, already? Ok, I... I'm coming..." stammered Dina

Dina turned then to the gentleman that she was dancing with and said:

"Well, thank you for the dance Grey..., It was quite enjoyable, but I must go now."

"It's Gavin," rectified the gentleman; "My name is Gavin. I had a wonderful time also," he added.

"Yeah Gavin," repeated Dina "So...good night." She added

Dina was turning to leave when Gavin uttered:

"Wait... Why don't you stay a little longer?"

"I'd like to, but they are my ride," said Dina, "and again, I have an appointment very early tomorrow." She added

At this precise moment, Julie who had left to pick up her present with Lucas returned, took Dina's hand and said while winkling her out:

"Sorry, but we need to go *now*!"

"In this case... can I at least have your phone number?" Asked Gavin

Dina suddenly realized how close she let this man approach her. Why does he need her phone number for? Maybe he thinks that he can charm her and enter in her life, and then cheat on her like Derrick did? "Never!" thought Dina, "I will never allow that to happen again. I must block him before he charms me, make me fall in love with him, and then abandon me for someone else."

Dina opened her mouth and replied: "It was just one dance damn it! I just wanted to have some fun tonight. I never want to see you again, you hear me?"

Gavin looked at Dina with astonishment, shook his head and asked: "Am I missing something here?"

"Yes, I don't date white men. I should have never accepted to dance with you!" Shouted Dina

"Unbelievable," replied Gavin.

Julie pressed Dina's hand slightly and said: "please Dina that's enough, let's go." Then, she turned to Gavin and stated:

"Please excuse her, sir; it's the effect of the alcohol. She is not used to drinking." Said Julie

"That's okay," replied Gavin, and, turning to Dina he added:

"Well, sorry if I offended you in any way, it was not my intention. Good night."

Lucas and Julie took Dina's hands and left with her. Once in the car, Julie turned to Dina and said: "That was a good thing that it was very noisy there, otherwise, people would have heard everything, and it would be more embarrassing for that guy. You were right not to want to drink alcohol, it makes you act crazy. And by the way, it was not just one dance, you two danced twice, and you seemed to really enjoy it."

Dina did not answer; she laid down in the back seat of the car and closed her eyes. When they dropped her at her house, Dina was so drunk that she couldn't walk properly; Julie and Lucas had to support her by her arms to help her go to her room where she collapsed in her bed and fell asleep.

Chapter 3

It was already 8 a.m. when Dina woke up. After praying to God, she took a quick shower; put on the clothes she had prepared for the occasion, combed her hair, and put a little makeup on her face. She grabbed her handbag and left her room to find her parents. "They must be awake by now," thought Dina. Her father is a manager at a hotel, he mostly works at night, while her mother is a homemaker. Dina found them sitting in the dining room, enjoying their breakfast quietly. When her mother saw her, she stated:

"Wow, you look beautiful baby girl."

"Thanks Mom," replied Dina, "can I borrow your car? I have to go to an important appointment this morning." Added Dina.

"Sure, you know where the keys are. But first you must sit down to eat your breakfast." Instructed her mother.

"Sorry mom, I don't have time for that; it's already eight thirty and my appointment is at nine." Replied Dina.

She was about to get the keys when her father said with his strong Haitian accent:

"Not so fast young lady! Can you tell us what kind of appointment you have that early in the morning?"

Dina was thinking, she didn't want to tell them about the job interview, she wanted to let them know only if she got hired. Because she knows how hard it was to find a job when you don't have any experience in the field, she didn't want to disappoint them again after the university episode. "But," thought Dina, "if I don't tell dad, he will not let me borrow the car."

"Oh, I forget to tell you, I have a job interview this morning at nine o'clock dad." Explained Dina

"That's great," said her mother, who stood up, and placed a sandwich and an apple in a lunch bag and handed it to Dina.

"Well," said her father, "in this case good luck."

"Thanks dad." Replied Dina

"By the way, how was the party last night with Julie?" Asked her father

"It was good, we had a lot of fun," answered Dina who didn't even remember how she got in her room last night."

Dina grabbed the car keys, opened the front door to leave, but, on the doorstep, she turned to her mother and said:

"Thanks, mom, for the breakfast."

"You're welcome," answered her mother with a smile.

Then, Dina closed the door behind her and rushed in the car. As soon as he saw her daughter getting in the car, Dina's dad turned to his wife and said:

"Do you think she's telling us the truth?"

"Why would she lie?" refuted his wife

"She was out last night with Julie, who knows what that girl and her friends had got her into, Julie is such a bad influence." Said her father

"Well it doesn't seem like her to keep secret from us" replied her mother.

"That was before she went away to the university, darling," stated her father. "You and I know perfectly that is not our innocent little girl who came back to us"; "obviously, something had happened to her" alleged her dad, "something that made her dropped out from the university and came back home, but more significantly, something so serious that she never even talked about with us."

"You're right" admitted her mother, "but let's see about this job interview, if it is true that she is looking for a job, she will find one sooner or later."

At this very moment, Ted got out of his room stretching his body.

"Did I hear your car leaving, or was I dreaming?" Ted asked his parents' while yawning.

"No, you weren't," confirmed his mother, "your sister just left for a job interview."

"Oh please, don't tell me that you are buying her lies? Since she came back, nothing interests her anymore, why would she be motivated enough to search for a job?" Inquired Ted

"Technically she never lied to us" retorted her father; "she just never tells us what had happened to her at the University campus."

"What difference does it make dad," responded Ted. "Just face it: Dina did not turn as well as you thought she would; your favorite child, who used to have good grades at school is not a lawyer, but an unemployed medical assistant who live with mom and dad."

"Just as her dumb little brother, what's the problem with that?" argued their father.

"The problem is that Dina messed up dad, she is not better than I, as you used to insinuate." insisted Ted

16

"She's still better than you," retorted his dad, "the proof is, she is out right now looking for a job to support herself, while you are standing here, in my house, trying to convince me that she is a pathological liar."

"In *your* house" repeated Ted, "I thought it was also *my* house, I can leave *your* house right now if you want me to." he added

"Enough!" shouted his mother. "Ted, you need to apologize to your father."

"Why should I apologize mom?" Asked Ted

"Because you're old enough to have your own place, you have to show respect to us if you want to stay here." Said his mother.

"But I didn't do anything wrong mom; anyway, I was already thinking about leaving, this house has become a court where I am the only person being prosecuted." Replied Ted

"And where would you stay? You do not have a job, neither a degree." Said his mother

"I could stay in Angel's house." Said Ted

"Your girlfriend's house? Nonsense! You are a Haitian born man, we do not live dependent on women, where is your pride?" shouted his dad.

"I was raised here in America, dad, I am not like you; I do not define what men and women should do or not. I consider relationship between two people equal in all sense. They are supposed to help each other for better and for worse." Replied Ted

"How are you planning to help her if she ever needs to pay her bills? Because trust me, once you start living with her, she might ask you to help cover the house expenses" Said his father

"Everything is about money with you; a real relationship is constructed on more than that, dad." Replied Ted

"For your sake, I hope that you are right, son." Concluded his father.

Ted went in his room and slammed the door behind him. He took one of his luggage and started putting his clothes in it. After it got full, he took another one and placed more clothes in it until it got full. After taking most of his things, he called Angel, who came and picked him up joyfully.

His dad, seeing him leaving home for good with his girlfriend, turned to his wife and asked: "What did we do wrong with these kids? My daughter came back home without achieving her dream of becoming a lawyer, and now, my son is leaving my house without neither a profession nor a job."

"It's not our fault," assured his wife. "This is just the way that children are now. We did everything that we could to help them succeed; they just don't understand it yet. Hopefully, Dina is now on the right path with her associate degree. Let's hope that Ted will also find his way back to school."

"You're right" replied Dina's father. He kissed his wife and went to his room.

Dina arrived at the office a quarter before nine. She located the facility easily, but she had trouble finding an empty parking space. She had to drive around for about ten minutes to wait for a car to leave. The lobby was filled with people waiting to see their Doctors. She went to the receptionist, an elderly Spanish woman, and presented herself:

"Good morning, my name is Dina Joseph. I have an appointment today with Doctor...One moment please...," said Dina

Suddenly, Dina realized that she didn't have the Doctor's name, but, fortunately, she brought a copy of the email that she had received. She opened her handbag, took the paper, and handed it to the receptionist and added:

"Actually...I received this email and it doesn't really have a Doctor's name on it, but only the office address."

"Oh, you're here for an interview for the medical assistant position?" asked the receptionist, while looking at the paper.

"Yes," answered Dina.

"Doctor Lawrence is waiting for you, let me take you to his office." She opened one of the drawers of her desk and took a folder on which was written "D. Joseph's Resume.

The receptionist stood up and invited Dina to follow her. She walked towards an alley to the right and found herself in front of a closed door. Dina who was following her noted the inscription on the door: Dr. G. Lawrence, Obstetrician/Gynecologist. The receptionist knocked lightly twice at the door and a deep masculine voice responded: "Come in." The receptionist told Dina to wait for a minute, opened the door, entered the room, and left the door partly open. Dina heard her saying:

"Ms. Joseph, the medical assistant, has arrived for the interview. Here's her resume, I already check her references."

"Thank you, Edna, you can bring her in," replied the deep voice.

Soon, the receptionist returned to Dina and said: "You can come in." Dina entered in the room followed by Edna; she found herself face to face with the man she had danced with the night before, in a white coat, sitting behind a big brown desk…

Chapter 4

"Oh no," thought Dina, "it cannot be true, not him. He is not going to give me the job."

"Thank you, Edna, you can return to your desk now," said the Doctor.

The receptionist left the room and closed the door behind her.

"Have a seat," said the Doctor, while showing her one of the chairs that were in front of him.

Dina couldn't move her feet, she was so surprised.

"Still drunk this morning," mocked the Doctor.

"No, I... I'm really sorry about last night," started Dina who was still standing near the door.

Seeing that she did not move, he said: "listen, there are many patients who are waiting, and my associate is on vacation, if you want us to have this interview, you better have a seat, so we can start."

Dina went quickly to sit down in the chair he had indicated to her. He cast a rapid glance at her resume. Dina looked at him, he seemed impassive.

"I understand that you just graduated, what types of procedures have you done on your internship?" asked Doctor Lawrence

"I recorded patients' medical histories and vital signs; I also collected their blood and urines samples and fulfilled office's tasks such as answering phones and ordering supplies. In addition, I managed insurance information." Replied Dina

"Why do you want to work here?" asked Doctor Lawrence

"Well, it is close to where I live, and it's a full-time position..." replied Dina

"Tell me Mrs. Joseph, why should I hire you?" asked Doctor Lawrence

"I know I gave you the wrong impression last night but, I'm very responsible, hardworking, and reliable. I have the skills and the training in Obstetrics/Gynecology procedures. On top of these, I'm fluent in Kreyol and French, I must mention that I just heard two of your patients speaking Kreyol in the waiting room." Replied Dina

"Speaking of patients, we have individuals from all ethnic groups here, and as I recall, you are a racist who doesn't like to do business with people who look like me. How do you plan to deal with those patients?" He asked, "because I'm warning you, I will not tolerate any type of prejudice against my patients here, especially racial prejudice, which is my number one preoccupation in this case." He added

"I knew it," thought Dina, 'he will not hire me. He brought up this subject just as a reason to turn me down."

"I apologize if I had said anything that made you think that I'm a racist, which I'm not. I completely understand your concerns," replied Dina. She stood up and added "Thank you for your time anyway..."

"I am not finished," he said in a harsh tone. If you are fair and kind towards all my patients, I won't really bother to know that you don't like them because of their skin color... Will you be fair and kind to all of my patients Ms. Joseph?" He asked

"Of course, I will..." promised Dina

"Anyway, Edna told me that you have two excellent references. Your professors have spoken highly of you. It appeared that you even graduated with honors. I have heard very good things about your skills and your character too, so I would like to give you a try; when can you start, if I hire you?" He asked

"Today if possible," answered Dina, very surprised but happy.

"Well, I'm an associate at this practice, we are two physicians, and each of us is supposed to have his own medical assistant. My partner already has Edna so... if hired you'll be specifically assigned to me, is that ok with you? He asked

"Of course," affirmed Dina.

"We are open Monday to Friday, from 8:00 a.m. to 5: 00 p.m. You'll start for fifteen dollars an hour, with benefits package such as: Full medical, dental and vision coverage. We also paid time off. Are you willing to start for the fifteen dollars an hour?" he queried

"I would work even for free, just to gain the experience, so I think fifteen dollars is okay for me to start." Avowed Dina

"One last important thing: Both you and Edna must do back and front office duties. You two can switch on a weekly basis or from time to time during the day, but it is vital for you to know there is no specific functions for you and Edna, as both of you are medical assistants for this office." He explained.

He cast a glance at his watch, stood up, held out his hand and congratulated Dina. She could not believe she had the job. He was shaking her hands and was congratulating her! Dina was thrilled.

"Thank you Doctor," said Dina

"Do you have any questions? Asked Doctor Lawrence

"I think you just told me everything I needed to know," replied Dina

Instantaneously, he looks at Dina straight in the eyes and said: "really?"

"I think so," replied Dina, troubled, "I mean... I think we covered everything I should know," added Dina.

"Well, I'm running behind schedule, so I'll take you to Edna, she will guide you around the office," said Doctor Lawrence.

Doctor Lawrence then led Dina to Edna who gives her some paperwork to fill, while explaining that she was on training for the day, and that there was no contract between the office and her yet and showed her where the supplies were.

"Now," said Edna, "you are going to help me with the patients. What size of clothes do you wear?"

"Well it depends on the brand," replied Dina, "but usually, I wear large on top and size fourteen for pants."

"That's what I thought," said Edna, who handed a red scrub to Dina.

Dina quickly went to the bathroom to change. While she was changing clothes, she thought about the interview, especially the ending part when Dr. Lawrence asked if she had any questions, the way he looked at her straight in the eyes and insisting as if he was insinuating something else with the "really" stuff. "No," thought Dina, "it's just one of these basic interview questions, it's probably because of what had happened at the nightclub last night that makes me think that."

When she returned, Edna told her to go in the examination rooms to take the patients vital signs as well as their chief complaint.

"Always remember to put the patient chart in the wall pocket outside the exam room door when you done with them," said Edna; "this way Doctor Lawrence will know which patient is ready for him to see. Don't forget to clean up the exam rooms after Dr Lawrence is done with each patient. We close the office for lunch at 1:00 p.m., and we reopen at 2:00, added Edna. You can stay inside to eat your lunch if you brought any, otherwise, you can go out to eat."

Before leaving, Edna added: "I'll be at the front office if you need me."

On her break, Dina borrowed the office's phone and called her parents to give them the news. Her mother and father were thrilled to learn that she was hired. Once she finished to talk to them, Dina went to the office parking lot, and sat inside her parent's car to eat the sandwich and the apple that her mother had given to her.

After eating the sandwich, Dina was thirsty. She went outside of the office and spotted a convenience store in the corner of the street. Dina walked to the store and bought a bottle of water. Once at the checkout counter, she placed the water in front of the cashier. "One dollar, and ninety-seven cents," said the cashier. Dina pulled out a dollar bill and fifty cents from her pockets. She gingerly checked her pants' pockets to try to find more change, but her pockets were empty.

Dina was about to leave the bottle of water at the register, when someone behind her touched her arm and said: "give it to me; I'll take care of it."

"This voice sounds familiar," thought Dina, "Doctor Lawrence... oh no, not him, I'll be too embarrassed."

Dina turned and found out she was right; Doctor Lawrence was indeed standing right behind her. She handed him the bottle of water without saying a word, he laid it on the cashier's counter, and Dina noticed that he had bought a plate of salad and a pack of gum. He paid with a credit card, and they left the store. Once outside, he handed the bottle of water to Dina.

Although embarrassed, Dina thanked him and moved away quickly to return to the office. But he went after her and asked: "Why are you in such a hurry? You still have more than fifteen minutes break and the office is right at the corner." Dina looked at her watch and murmured: "yeah, you're right."

While walking along with Doctor Lawrence, Dina opened the bottle of water, and drank a sip. Doctor Lawrence opened the pack of gum and handed it to her; she took one and thanked him. Then, Dina unwrapped the gum, and put it in her mouth, she immediately felt the minty flavor.

"Great chewing gum. It gives a fresh taste to my mouth." Said Dina

"Yeah, you seem all tensed up, it will help you feel relaxed too. So, how is your first day of work?" asked Doctor Lawrence.

"Pretty good, I learned a lot today." Replied Dina

"Well, Edna told me that you help a lot too. You still don't have any questions?" asked Doctor Lawrence

"Actually, I do, I forgot to ask you about the office's policies." Said Dina

"Hmm... Very important, I will give you a copy of the manual today before you leave. I'm glad that you asked. Is that all?" Asked Doctor Lawrence.

"About last night..., I would like to apologize. I was drunk and I wasn't thinking clearly." Said Dina.

"Apology accepted." Replied Doctor Lawrence.

Doctor Lawrence and Dina arrived at the office building; he opened the door and let Dina pass before him.

"Thank you!" said Dina.

"See you around" he replied while walking toward his office.

The day was very busy and went by quickly. Before leaving, Dina checked that all the exam rooms were clean, and went to see Edna.

"It was a tough day," said Edna. "For a new employee, you handled it very well; I am really impressed," added Edna

"Well thank you, Edna, I was really eager to find a job, I guess that explains why I am able to manage it." Replied Dina.

"Maybe; anyway, I'm glad that Doctor Lawrence allowed you to start your training today. From what I see, the office is going to function smoothly. Doctor Lawrence wants to see you before you leave, he's in his office." Said Edna

"Okay, I'm going to see him right now" Replied Dina.

Why does Doctor Lawrence want to see me before I leave? Did he change his mind about hiring me? Thought Dina

Once in front of Doctor Lawrence's office, Dina took a deep breath. She couldn't decide herself to knock at the door… She was still standing behind the door when she heard a now familiar voice behind her whispering:

"Is that so much inconvenient for you to enter in my office?"

It was Doctor Lawrence… again. Dina felt so embarrassed by this question, but hurried to answer:

"Not at all, I was just thinking about how to apologize again for last night."

"You already did," replied Doctor Lawrence. "Now, what about we get inside my office to finish this discussion?" He added while opening his door to let Dina in.

"Sure," replied Dina who enter inside his office. He enters after her, closes the door, and went to sitt on his elegant chair.

"Please have a seat. I'm not going to hold you longer, I just wanted you to have the policies manual, and have your signature on these agreements papers. You also need to fill out the tax papers and bring them back tomorrow," said Doctor Lawrence while handing the papers to Dina.

"Oh, I completely forget about them. Thank you for reminding me." Replied Dina

She sat down in a chair in front of his desk, picked a pen, and started signing the agreement papers.

"Well, they must not be that important for you. You seem to be the kind of person that usually remembers things." Said Doctor Lawrence.

Dina knows that he was referring to the regrettable conversation that she had with him last night, when she told him how much she missed her ex and was unable to get over him. Also, the way she treated him like he was responsible for what her ex did to her, and she felt ashamed. At this moment, she wished that she had never put her feet in the Antillean nightclub.

"I'm sorry that I had this regrettable conversation with you last night; trust me, I wish that none of this had ever happened. I know how awful I was, and if it was possible, I would start *everything* differently. But it's not possible; all I can do is apologize and try to prove to you that I'm not a bad person. Last night, I just got caught in an unpleasant situation." Explained Dina.

"Really?" asked Doctor Lawrence.

"Really, I'm not a bad person." Retorted Dina

"I mean really, you would start *everything* differently if it was possible?" asked Doctor Lawrence

"Yes," responded Dina, "but as I said…" she continued

"Hold on, if you really want a fresh start, we can go to the nightclub together tonight." Proposed Dr. Lawrence

"You would go in this nightclub with me after what had happened the night before?" Asked Dina, surprised.

"Why not? You said it yourself: you were drunk; I would like to see you dancing and chatting when you are not intoxicated." Replied Doctor Lawrence

"I don't think it is a good idea to go out together now that I'm working for you." Said Dina

"You mean that if I wanted you to go out with me, I shouldn't hire you?" Asked Doctor Lawrence

"No, I mean… last night you were a stranger; now that you are my employer, I don't want to… to…" stuttered Dina

"To insult me again in front of a crowd?" Asked Doctor Lawrence, amused.

"I would never do that… again." Stammered Dina

"Well, you might have to prove it. I bet that you can't, because you are not sorry enough…Do you want to take the bet and prove me wrong?" Whispered Doctor Lawrence with a smile.

"I… I think I will take the bet." Replied Dina hesitant.

"Tonight, at nine, same place," said Doctor Lawrence with a firm voice.

"Oh, I'm sorry but tonight is not a good time, maybe tomorrow." Explained Dina

"Sure, you had a busy day, you must be tired. See you tomorrow then." Said sadly Doctor Lawrence.

Dina felt sorry for him, it sounds like he was really looking forward on going out tonight.

"No, it's not because I'm tired; it just that I usually borrow my parents' car, and tonight, they have to go to their weekly prayer meeting." Explained Dina.

"If it is the case, I could pick you up." Proposed Doctor Lawrence.

"That would be great. My address is in my application. Do you want me to write it in a different sheet of paper for you?" Asked Dina

"Sure," replied Doctor Lawrence; "here, write it on my address book," he added while handing a notebook to her.

Dina took the address book, wrote her home address in it, and handed it back to him.

"So, see you at nine o'clock then." Said Doctor Lawrence

"Nine o'clock," confirmed Dina, who picked up the papers and left.

She went to change the scrubs against her clothes and picked up her handbag. Then, she searched for Edna, and found her sitting in the waiting room.

"I was waiting for you," said Edna as Dina was approaching. "Is everything all right?" she added

"Yes" answered Dina, "I had some papers to sign."

"I see" replied Edna, who stood up, and grabbed her handbag; "I just wanted to be sure that he did not change his mind about hiring you. You did such a good job today, as I said, I am impressed by how well you work. It's been a long time that I didn't work with someone as devoted as you." Added Edna, who opened the exit door, and got out of the building, following by Dina.

"Well, I think that we are going to work together for a long time; I just signed the agreement papers, so I'm officially hired." Indicated Dina

"Good," replied Edna. "See you tomorrow then," she added with a smile while working towards her car.

"See you tomorrow," replied Dina.

Dina got into her car and put her handbags in the passenger's front seat. She locked the doors, fixed the mirrors, and started the car. After looking behind the car, she looked rapidly around her and left the office parking, in direction of her parents' house. While driving, a song came to her mind:
"Thanks be to God I found a job
Now I can go to shop
Afford my own place
And finally save face.
I'm going to have a paycheck
At last a promising prospect."

Chapter 5

D ina arrived at her house a few minutes later. She went straight to the half bathroom near the family room to wash her hands. Her mother was in the laundry room, she went to kiss her, and they talked about her first day at work. Her mother told her how proud she was of her, finding a job soon after her graduation.

Dina's father was taking a shower, and when he finished, he came to Dina, as she was eating the fried banana with the goat meat that her mother had prepared in the kitchen. Dina's father congratulated her on her new job also and asked about the rest of the staff. "We were three working at the office today, but Doctor Lawrence said that he has a partner who he is actually out of state and will probably come back in a few days."

"Well," said Dina's father, "I'm glad that you found this job; you were a brilliant student, and you deserve it."

"Thanks dad," replied Dina. "I'm really tired, I think I'm going to get some rest."

"Okay," said her father, see you later."

"By the way, where is Ted? I can't wait to share this good news with him," said Dina as she was leaving the table. Realizing that neither of them responded, Dina turned towards her parents, waiting for an answer, but instead of responding, her parents looked at each other and exchanged a knowing look. Finally, her father stated that they will have this conversation after she gets some rest.

"That's weird," thought Dina as she walked towards her room, "why can't they talk to me about my little brother? He surely got into an argument with dad again, that's why mom and dad don't want to talk about him."

Dina went to her room and closed her door, she kneeled, bowed her head, and thanked God for allowing her to find the job. Then, she put on her sleepwear, and went to bed: she fell too tired to take a shower. "I will take a shower when I wake up" thought Dina, who felt asleep right away.

The door bell ringing woke her up. She stood up and went to see who it was.

"Mom! Dad!" Shouted Dina, "someone is knocking at the door."

As no one answered, Dina decided to check if they were in the living room. Seeing that the TV was not turned on, Dina realized that her parents must be out, otherwise, they would be sitting together on the large brown couch watching their favorite show: *Love After Fifty,*" which should be ended at nine.

"*Prayer Meeting!*" remembered Dina, "they have prayer meeting this evening; maybe they had already left." At the same time, someone rang the doorbell again. "I'm coming!" said Dina who went into the living room, were there is a better view of the front house and looked at the window. Doctor Lawrence was standing in front of the door.

"Oh no," thought Dina, "I forgot about him. What time is it? What time is it?" She asked herself. She turned her head, and looked at the clock, it was 9:15; "I'm not prepared to go out! Where are my parents? Why didn't they wake me up? It doesn't sound like them leaving the house without informing me."

"Mom! Dad!" yelled Dina, as she walked towards her parents' room. She hoped that they were still at home. Once in front of their door, Dina knocked at it, no one answered the door. Dina touched the door handle and realized that the door wasn't locked, she opened it and entered the room. Seeing a bunch of clothes on the bed, she headed towards the bathroom. "Mom! Dad!" Shouted Dina, while walking towards the bathroom, to see if either one of them where there. The bathroom door was open; she cast a glance inside it, and, seeing that it was empty, left their room to go in her brother's room.

At the same time, the bell at the entrance door rang again. "Ted!" Shouted Dina, as she knocked on his room's door, "can you please get the door for me?" Not hearing any response from Ted, she opened his door and was stupefied: her brother's room was practically empty, only his bed and the drawers were left.

"I'm alone, mom and dad must have already left for the church meeting," realized Dina. "Let me just let him in, and then I will go to prepare myself."

As Dina walked towards the front door, she realized that she was still wearing her sleepwear. She was about to go back to change herself when she heard Doctor Lawrence saying:

"I can see your silhouette you know; I know that's you because your parents' car is not here. You can either open the door or ask me to go away if you have changed your mind."

Dina opened the door immediately and let him in. He entered and followed Dina without saying a word. She brought him into the living room. Then, seeing that he was looking at her clothes, she explained: "I'm sorry, I fell asleep, that's why I'm not ready yet. You can sit down for a minute while I will go to take a quick shower," concluded Dina while handing the TV remote to him. He took the television remote and sat down on the couch. "I'm sure you will find something interesting to watch while I'm getting ready" she asserted, while heading to her room.

"Do you have anything specials that you could recommend to me? What do you usually watch at this hour?" asked Doctor Lawrence.

"I do have a few, but... you would not like any of them," replied Dina, as she was still walking towards her room.

"You never know; just give me a suggestion of any of your favorite TV programs and I will try it." Said Doctor Lawrence.

Dina was already inside her room when she heard him stating that he wanted her to give him a suggestion of what to watch. She couldn't decide between staying in her room to take a shower and going back to the living room to help him find one of her favorite shows to watch. "We are already late," thought Dina, "why doesn't he just watch anything and let me prepare myself rapidly? I'm just going to take a shower." She was about to take off her pajamas, when she changed her mind: "I better go to help him find an interesting program to watch, after all, I'm the one who was not ready on time."

Without further delay Dina returned to the living room. She found Doctor Lawrence, remote in hand, watching a show called *"Former Lovers Reunion."*

"Oh, I see that you have found something." Said Dina

"Indeed," he answered, "it was auto programmed. Apparently, someone really like this show and didn't want to miss it." Assumed Doctor Lawrence.

Dina felt embarrassed; obviously he suspected that was her who auto programmed it. He must think that she is a depressed woman, who never gets over her cheater boyfriend, and still dream about him coming back; and worse, he must think that she is obsessed about getting him back. "Anyway," thought Dina, "that's my business not his; if my private life does not have a repercussion in my job performance, it should not be a concern to him."

"Yes, I am an unconditional fan of this show." Avowed Dina haughtily. "I auto programmed it because it starts right after my parents' favorite show. They tend to search for other programs and make me miss it; therefore, I had to auto-programmed it." Admitted Dina.

"Me too," said Doctor Lawrence with a smile, "this is one of my favorite shows."

Seeing the surprised expression on her face, Doctor Lawrence added:

"You know, if you did not have all those prejudices, you would realize that people from all racial backgrounds can be sensitive."

Dina could not believe it, Doctor Lawrence, this handsome and successful man who likes nightclubs, also like to watch romantic television shows.

"So, what about we stay here to watch this show? I was anxious to miss it, and I think you would like to watch it too." Said Doctor Lawrence.

Dina acquiesced. She sat in a couch opposed to the one that he was sitting on and started watching the episode.

The show always features former lovers that came back together, and tonight, they were featuring a couple that were separated for about three years and who have decided to give their relationship another try.

On this segment, the couple agreed to meet up at their favorite restaurant. The lady came first, and five minutes later, the gentleman made his entrance. They smiled at each other, and then the man approached the woman's table and kissed her on the cheek. He sat down in front of her and said:

"You didn't change at all, always on time."

"You did not change either," replied the lady with a smile, "always late."

At the same time, a server arrived and handed them the menu.

While they were looking at the menu, the server asked them if they wanted to drink something in the meantime.

"Yes," answered the gentleman, "can you bring us a bottle of fruity white champagne in this range, please," he added while pointing to a price on the menu list, "we are celebrating tonight."

The server left, and after a few minutes, he came back with a bottle of champagne. He served the lady first, and then he served the guy.

"We are ready to order now," said the gentleman.

The server took his pen and his notepad from his pocket, wrote their order and left.

They were finally alone, and the guy took the opportunity to tell his lady how happy he was that she had accepted to see him ultimately.

"I'm still in love with you," said the guy. "I know I'm the only one to blame for our breakup, because I wasn't an exemplary husband, but I promise you that if you give me another chance, I will do everything I can to make you happy."

"You are not the only one to blame," answered the lady; "I should have been more supportive. I thought that you didn't love me anymore, so I stopped fighting for our love."

"I never stopped loving you; I'm lost without you," said the guy while taking the lady's hands. He gently rubbed the back of her hands, and then kissed them. After he finished kissing her hands, he went close to her face, and he pressed his lips against hers.

The server arrived with their order, and Dina jumped when she heard a voice saying: "I think that they have the same taste when it comes to food, they both ordered rice and chicken." She turned her head in Doctor Lawrence's direction, and looked back at the tv; she noticed that Doctor Lawrence was right; they both ordered the same dish.

"This show is so interesting that I forget that Doctor Lawrence was here," taught Dina. The couple were eating their food now, and Dina remembered that she forgets to offer something to drink to him. She got up and asked him if he wanted to drink some juice.

"Don't bother, he said, I'm not really thirsty, but I'm hungry," he added while standing. "I think that I'm going home."

Dina felt ashamed because she forgot to offer him a drink.

"I can fix you something quickly you know." Proposed Dina

"Really" answered Doctor Lawrence, "I didn't think that you knew how to cook" he said while looking at her perfectly done nails.

"Well," answered Dina," it is often said that appearance is misleading. And never underestimate a Haitian-American girl with long nails."

He smiled, but refused to let her cook, pretending that she was going to miss the end of the show.

"I am already satisfied with what I saw," said Dina, "there's no doubt that they are soon going to be reconciled."

Right away, Dina went to the kitchen, and took some cod, soaked it in tap water, then she took two plantains, washed them, cut off both ends, and sliced the skins lightly lengthwise without peeling them. After that, she put the plantains in a pot, poured half cup of water and added a pinch of salt in the water before boiling the plantains. Then, she took the cod from the tap water, passed it in one teaspoon of apple cider vinegar and one half of lemon juice, rinsed it, and fried it in a buttered saucepan. After two minutes, Dina added one teaspoon of tomato paste to the buttered cod.

After two more minutes, Dina added two cups of water, one chicken bouillon cube, and half teaspoon of Haitian spice, made of garlic, green onions, cloves, and black pepper to the cod. Finally, she added half of a green bell pepper, one spicy pepper, and one sprig of parsley tied with a sprig of thyme in the cod and brought it to boil. Lastly, Dina added a medium red onion sliced in the sauce and turn it off.

Once the food was ready, Dina peeled the plantains skin's, and placed the plantains on a white oval platter; she also poured the cod sauce on a deep angled porcelain sauce dish. Then, she placed the food over the dining room table, and went to Doctor Lawrence, and asked him to follow her to the dining room to eat.

Doctor Lawrence stood up and followed Dina. She served him one plantain with some cod sauce, then, she showed him the two kinds of juices that she had in the refrigerator and asked him which one he preferred to drink first between the pineapple and the orange juice. He chose the pineapple; "that's the one I prefer too," avowed Dina. After they ate, he thanked her, and said that the food was delicious.

"This is the first time that I have eaten Haitian food, it is very tasty," said Doctor Lawrence.

"Thank you, Doctor Lawrence, this is a simple and fast meal to cook, I always make it when I'm in a hurry," said Dina, happy to know that he liked her food.

"Please call me Gavin," said Doctor Lawrence.

Dina acquiesced. After that, they went back to the living room, but Dina noticed that the local evening newscasts were on and the show was over.

"Have you seen the end of the show?" asked Dina.

"Yeah," replied Gavin

"Did they get back together as expected?" she asked.

"Yes" he answered, "as it always ends most of the time in this show" he added.

"This is a good thing," asserted Dina

"So, you really think that partners who are separated should get back together, instead of seeing new people and start over again?" Asked Gavin

"I believe it is more prudent to know who you are dealing with, and a former partner is a safer bet than a new one. At least, you already know his flaws." Explained Dina

"You mean you would go back to someone who broke your heart and would probably break it again, because in your opinion it's "*safer?*" Wow, you really need some therapy Dina!" Retorted Gavin.

"I wasn't talking about me… stammered Dina," ashamed to have let her feelings being so obvious.

"But you do think it is safer to take back a former boyfriend because you can predict his next move, right?" Argued Gavin.

"Personally, yes. I think it's safer." Admitted Dina.

Gavin gave Dina a disapproving look and said:

"Safer? How's that?" he asked.

"Because as you said, you already know the problem that you are going to face with the person that you know and would be better prepared to undertake and resolve them than the ones that you would encounter with a new partner." Explained Dina.

"Do you realize what you just said: "I am ready to give my heart back to someone who already broke it, knowing that it is likely that this person would hurt me again, just because I am too afraid to give my heart to someone who has not and would probably never break it." Said Gavin.

Dina found nothing to say for her defense; it was what she meant to say, but not with such harsh words.

Seeing that Dina could not answer, Gavin announced:

"Well I think it is time for me to go."

"We can search for another show that you might like," suggested Dina nervously.

"No, enough show for me tonight. I think I'd rather go home instead of listening to someone who takes pleasure at being a victim," said Gavin as he stood up.

"I thought you loved this show?" Asked Dina, surprised.

"Yes, I like to watch it, but I don't want to *live* it. You see, you and I are watching it for completely distinct reasons Ms. Joseph."

"Please, call me Dina, I'm your employee after all." Said Dina.

"Well Dina, I watch that show to entertain myself, while you are watching it because you identify yourself with some of the characters. I think you should take a chance and try something new. You want to go back to your old ways because you are too scared to start over. You actually think this is the way it's supposed to be; I can't believe this is the kind of relationship that you want to have with someone." Said Gavin

"Not everybody gets another option, you know; you are lucky if you had never been stuck with someone that you really love," said sadly Dina. She felt a tear getting down her cheek and wiped it away with her right hand. She looked at her hand and saw that they were dyed black. "The mascara" remembered Dina, I didn't remove my makeup nor take a shower before sleeping. Embarrassed, Dina quickly closed her eyes and bowed her head.

When Dina opened her eyes a few seconds later, Doctor Lawrence was in front of her. He took her right hand in his hands and said while rubbing it:

"I'm sorry to have been so hard on you, but remember, there's always another option; you just have to find it. Trust me, you have so much to offer that you don't have to take back someone who broke your heart and therefore does not deserve you."

After Gavin finished to massage Dina's hand, he let it go. Dina looked, and discovered that the mascara that was melted with her tear was erased from her hand. Gavin kissed her tenderly on her forehead and wished her a good night. Then, he walked to the front door and opened it. He went out and closed the door behind him.

Dina stood still, she could not move; for the first time since Derrick had left her, she cried. She felt relieved and free at the same time.

Chapter 6

The doorbell ring surprised her. It's probably Doctor Lawrence thought Dina; He surely came back to apologize again. But, as a precaution, she looked through the window before opening. At her big surprise, it was Julie that was standing there, and Gavin's car was gone. Relieved and a little disturbed at the same time, Dina went to open for Julie.

"I cannot go out tonight Julie, from now one, you'll have to deal with your parents, I have to go to work early tomorrow morning…" announced Dina, "Sorry, but from now one, you're on your own girl…" she added

"I am not going out tonight either," replied Julie, "and I am not here for that. My parents said that you had company tonight. Apparently, they saw you open the door for a man since nine o'clock and it appears that they just saw him leaving a few minutes ago. Since they know that you were alone, they sent me to see if you were okay"

"Although my parents are not here, how did you know that I was alone? Ted might have been here." Said Dina

"I know that your brother is not here Dina, we saw him moving out with his stuff this morning." Replied Julie

Dina couldn't believe what she heard; the long-time neighbors and friends of her family were snooping on them. They knew everything that was going on inside her house.

"I just came to see if you were okay," maintained Julie

"Well thank you for your concern, but as you can see, I'm fine." Declared Dina

"Yeah, I can see that you are fine," said Julie while looking at Dina in her pajamas.

"This is not what you think," said Dina, "it was just my new employer."

"Your new employer?" repeated Julie incredulous, "that's very interesting… and what was he doing in your house at this time?" She asked.

Dina suddenly realized how it would be complicated to explain all of this to Julie. "You know what, said Dina, I'm really tired, it would be better if you go home; I promise that I will explain everything to you during this week-end."

"No, no," insisted Julie while sitting on a chair, "I want to know now. I cannot wait until this week-end to hear about this strange story."

Instantaneously, the entry door closed, and Dina's parents walked towards Julie and her.

"What strange story are you asking about, Julie?" asked Dina's mother.

Dina realized that she was so focused in her dialogue with Julie that she did not heard her parents' car coming, nor the keys opening the door.

"Oh, Dina told me that she has to wake up early to go to work tomorrow, and I was like: that's a strange story, I did not know that you had found a job," lied Julie who stood up immediately, wished a goodnight to them, and left.

"Why is Ted's room empty?" asked Dina to her parents after Julie had left.

Her mother sat down on the couch, bowed her head as she didn't want to look at her husband and said: "your brother has moved out."

Dina collapsed on a chair.

"Moved out?" repeated Dina incredulous, "But why? I mean I suspected that you guys have gotten into an argument but why it is so serious that he had to move out? And where did he go?" asked Dina.

"Like you said, He got into an argument with me, but he had voluntary decided to leave," replied her dad.

Dina could not believe it. Her brother who's not working had left home just like that? it was too much for her to bear. Ted never wanted to leave home, he would had never left if her dad wasn't pushing him away; all Ted had ever wanted was to stay in his parents' house and enjoy life with his friends.

Dina stood up and asked her parents for the second time if they knew where her brother was.

"He said he will stay at his girlfriend's house," responded her father.

"I'm going to get him" she announced. She took the car keys, and headed to exit the door, but her mother grabbed her by her wrist and murmured:

"There is something that you need to know before you go."

Dina looked alternately at her mother and her father. "What is it?" She asked exasperated.

Her mother then looked at her father, who immediately bowed his head. "The argument was about you," confessed finally her father." "He thought that you were lying about your job interview." He added.

"But why would Ted think like that about me?" asked Dina.

"You must admit that you have changed since you came back home from Colossal University, Dina; you never talked about what happened to you there, what had hurt you so much that you had to drop out of this expensive law school that had already consumed most of our money."

"So, he left home because of me, somehow, a dispute had broken between you guys mostly because of me," figured Dina gloomily.

"No, it is not your fault that your brother wanted me to admit that he is better than you." said her father. "It is obvious that you had made some mistakes when you went to that university, but I wasn't there to protect you, and at least you had tried." he added.

"I'm sorry that this time I'm the cause of your disagreement. Now, I'm going to try to persuade him to come back home." said firmly Dina.

"Don't count too much on making him change his mind; I don't want you to be deceived; you know how your brother is so stubborn," Said her mother.

Dina parked her car in front of Angel's house, she knows this house like the back of her hand, for she had been there a few times when she and Ted were teenagers. Angel's family was also from Haiti. Michel, Angel's brother was in the same basketball team as Ted, and they often organized parties where Dina was also invited.

Angel and Michel were from two different mothers. Because their father did not marry either of their mothers, he could not apply for either of these women to rejoin him when he submitted the application for Angel and Michel. While their single father was often at work, Angel and Michel were always alone at home. They could have friends over and organize parties as much as they wanted. They grow up without any strict parental control as opposite to Dina and Ted, whose mother was always at home, while their father was the only bread winner. Angel's mother often sent her pictures of herself, and the photos of the other children she had with another man.

As for Michel, he never had any contact with his mother since he came to rejoin his dad when he was just seven years old.

It was the only house where Dina went to some of the rare parties that she had ever attended. Since she's a girl in a Haitian household, her parents did not want her to go to parties. But Ted, even though he was younger than Dina, was always allowed to attend every party that he was invited to. Dina could go to a party only if her brother vouched to their parents that he would watch her closely. Given all the familial restrictions that she had to face because of her gender when she had to go out, Dina always accepted Angel's family parties' invitation with pleasure.

Dina locked the car and walked up the stairways towards the door. She knocked on the door, and a few minutes later, Angel opened and let her in.

"Hi Dina, how are you?" asked Angel with her sharp voice.

"I'm good," answered Dina "I just came to talk to Ted, I heard he might be here, is he?"

"He's here, but he told me that he does not want to see any of you." Said Angel

"Could you please tell him that I'm here?" argued Dina

"Ted knows that you're here Dina, because he saw you from my room window's; he sent me instead because he just doesn't want to talk to you." Replied Angel

Dina was frustrated, all she wanted was to talk face to face to her brother and convince him to come back home. But, apparently, Angel was determinate to keep her from seeing him.

"Well, if it is the way he wants it, I'm okay with that," said Dina as she stood up. She closed her eyes and took a deep breath.

"Are you okay?" asked Angel

"Yes," answered Dina

"I'm really sorry about all of this, I know how it is affecting you, but I assure you that Ted will be okay here." Said Angel.

"Oh, I don't have any doubt about that." retorted Dina.

"Is there anything that I can do for you?" asked Angel impatient to get rid of Dina

"Now that you've asked, I would appreciate a glass of water, please." said Dina.

"Sure" replied Angel who invited Dina to sit down again. "I'm going to get it for you" she added.

Once Angel left the living room and went to the kitchen to get her the glass of water, Dina profited to go to Angel's room and to try to talk to Ted. She found Angel's room without any difficulties, as she used to come in it to use the bathroom when they had parties. She entered the room without knocking on the door, and found Ted lying in Angel's bed, eyes closed, with a big headphone on his head, listening to music and singing. Dina touched Ted's shoulder, and he opened his eyes. When Ted saw Dina standing near the bed, he jumped up.

"Oh, look who's here, the perfect child! what do you want Dina?" he asked perplexed.

"I heard what happened at home, and I came here to talk to you." Replied Dina

"I don't have anything to say to you, go home," said Ted

"Why? What did I do to you Ted, why are you so mad at me for?"

He looked at Dina with surprise and repeated Dina's words: "What did you do to me?" then, he exclaimed "You don't know what you did to me? Well, let me tell you *what you did to me*: you are dad preferred child, when I'm not; you always get good grades at school, which I never had. On top of this, you wasted dad's money to study something that you never finished, and nobody never asked you a damn question about that. But, of course, dad is always there to remind me of what a loser I am; yes, me, who never earned a degree, and now, me who is not searching for a job."

Dina listened to him calmly.

"Wow, you had a lot there for me she said while touching her chest. But you still didn't tell me what I did to you, because you see," started Dina, "most of what you are blaming me for have nothing to do with me; they are just excuses that you have made to justify your hostility with dad. You are mom's favorite child, Ted; do I have to resent you for that? No! And you know what? You are right about me wasting daddy's money. I know I did that, I know that I messed up. If your problem is because you don't know why, I'm going to tell you: I am the real loser Ted, I'm not better than you. And… and… you know what? You are even better than me." Said Dina.

"I wasted daddy's money because I fell in love with a guy who played with my heart and then broke it," continued Dina.

She was crying now, she didn't care anymore that Ted knows about her big mistake who had cost her a lot, as long as it could keep him from messing up his own life.

"Yes, I was practically living in the same residence with that guy. He said that he would marry me as soon as he gets his medical license, but guess what? He was dating another girl while he was dating me and was probably telling her the same bogus; or maybe he did marry her, who knows. Anyway, I was betrayed and humiliated. This is the reason why I dropped from the university, and came back home, after wasting daddy's money. I hope that you are satisfied now that you know my story. Now, you can come home and tell dad yourself what kind of loser his daughter is, but please, come home Ted."

Seeing that he still didn't move, Dina continued:

"For many years, I dreamed about going to this university where I could be away from all of you; but once I got there, I realized how lucky I was to have my whole family in my entourage to protect me. I was happy to come home to find mom, dad, and you. Please Ted let's go home, don't act like me, by doing something that you could regret later. Trust me, if I had my family close enough to keep me away from that guy, today I would have something better than a minimum wage job".

"Good speech," said Angel, who suddenly appeared with a glass of water on her hand; "now get out of my room!"

"You don't talk to my sister like that" said Ted "she came here to see me."

"You told me that she was the reason why your dad threw you out" persisted Angel

"Yes, but she wasn't even there, it's not like it was her fault," explained Ted

"Well I'm sorry, but no family reunion in my room!" exclaimed Angel

"What do you mean Angel?" asked Ted

"What I mean is that you take your sister, and your broken ass, and get out of my house; you can't even afford your own place, and you want to impose your sister in my room. Don't tell me that you plan on making her move into my house also when your parents throw her out too. Everyone in this community knows that you and her are living from your parents' assets, which is a shame. I can deal with your broken ass here, but not hers." Argued Angel

"You are so pathetic Angel, I never knew that you could be so mean." exclaimed Ted. He grabbed a yellow shirt that was lying on the bed, put it on, and took his sister's hand. "Let's go Dina" he said.

"Yeah, go away" continued Angel while pursuing them.

Once Dina and Ted arrived in front of the entrance door, Angel pushed them out of her house, and slammed the door behind them.

They walked out the stairway towards the car, unlocked the doors, and sat inside to talk. Ted apologized to Dina and accepted to come back home. Dina drove until they reached their house. Inside the house, the lights were on, but their parents were already in bed, Ted went into the kitchen to eat, and Dina went to her room, brushed her teeth, and finally took a shower.

"It was a tough day" thought Dina, "but fortunately, everything went well at the end." After taking a shower, Dina went to her brother's room to say goodnight, she realized that he did not have a pillow, neither a draw sheet in his bed to sleep, she went in her room, and handed him a pair of her draw sheets.

"They are pink" complained Ted

"It just for one night, Ted, mom will give you some extra bedding tomorrow. Besides, the color won't bite you," joked Dina. Then, she wished Ted a goodnight, and went back to her room. There, Dina set the alarm clock on seven, and went to bed. She was so tired that she slept almost immediately.

Chapter 7

The alarm clock rang, and Dina jumped out of her bed. she brushed her teeth and took a shower. After that, she put on deodorant on her armpits, applied some lotion on her body, and put a pink dress. Then, she went to the kitchen, where she found her parents sitting, and eating their breakfast.

"Good morning," said Dina, "you were sleeping when we came home last night."

"We?" asked her dad, surprised.

"Yes dad, Ted is here; he came with me last night. Please be nice to him, I'm going to be late for work if I don't leave right now; see you tonight." Replied Dina

"Have a nice day," said her mother, who handed her a lunch bag.

"Thanks mom," said Dina. "Have a peaceful day," she added.

After getting her car parked in the office parking lot, Dina looked at her watch, and realized that she arrived a quarter before her schedule time. She took her handbag and her lunch, got out of her car, locked it, and finally, entered inside the office. Edna was already there, and Dina greeted her.

"Good morning, Dina" responded Edna. Today is going to be a busy day like yesterday, but mostly for us. Doctor Lawrence's partner is back, so he will have time to catch his breath between patients today. I felt sorry for him when I saw the number of patients, he had to consult all alone in the past weeks"

"He must feel relieved then," said Dina

"Oh, he never complained, he really loves what he's doing, but I know he's tired sometimes because his eyes are often red in the afternoon." Explained Edna

"Well I'm happy that he won't have to do all the work alone anymore," answered Dina. "I'm going to change my clothes, and I will be back to you in a minute." Replied Dina

"Okay," answered Edna.

Dina went in the cabinet, took the scrubs where she left them the day before. She then went to the bathroom to change. She got out of her dress and put on the pants; she was about to put on the skirt, when suddenly the bathroom door opened.

"It's busy!" exclaimed Dina. But it was too late, someone who seemed as surprised as her entered the bathroom. It was Derrick in flesh and bones...

"Dina?! I... I'm sorry," stammered Derrick. "I think that you forgot to lock the door. But what are you doing here?" He asked, then seeing the scrub pants, he added "you're working here, aren't you? You must be the new medical assistant that Gavin had hired."

Dina remained silent. She could not believe that she was in the same place, or better yet in the same bathroom as Derrick. He was the first love of her life, the man that she had dreamed about marrying one day; the man who also betrayed her and left her for another girl.

Seeing that Dina would not answer, Derrick decided to leave her alone.

"I just wanted to wash my hands, I think it's better that I go to do that in one of the examination room sinks," said Derrick "make sure that you lock that door this time," he added amused. "I will see you when you're done, we need to talk."

"We need to talk," repeated Dina mentally. "About what? He had probably married that brunette with whom he was cheating with, and therefore does not want me to work at his office. Well, suits me! because I do not want to work with him either."

Dina put on her dress again, folded the scrubs, and went to put them back where she took them. She walked quietly through the waiting room and was happy to see that Edna was not there. She took her handbag and was about to go outside when she heard Derrick's voice saying:

"Where are you going, Dina?" "Don't tell me that you are about to run away again?" He added. Dina did not answer, she continued to walk towards the exit door, but he followed her, and took her by her right arm and made her pivoted towards him.

"Come on Dina, you can't just walk out of your job like that." Said Derrick. "Edna told me how a devoted employee that you are. Look, I know that I'm the reason why you do not want to stay here, so I'm going to take the day off, until I found a way to deal with this issue, okay." Seeing that she still had not moved, he added gently: "Please Dina, go back to your job."

Dina freed her arm, looked at him straight in the eyes and declared: "what about Doctor Lawrence, huh? He was overwhelmed yesterday, and Edna told me this morning that we are expecting the same number of patients today. You cannot take the day off; I'm the one who should go."

Dina walked to her car, but he followed her and grabbed her right arm again." Why don't both of us stay and do our job? I promise that I won't bother you. Besides, I don't think it would be fair to Gavin if any of us left."

"He's right," thought Dina. She agreed and followed him back to the office.

"I was searching for you," said Edna; "I see that you've already made acquaintance with Doctor Lee." She added.

Dina pretended that she did not hear what Edna had said, but Derrick immediately replied:

"Dina and I know each other very well."

"Oh, really?" Asked Edna, intrigued.

"We went to the same university." Explained Dina.

"We also shared the same dormitory, thanks to the gender-neutral housing program of our university," continued Derrick, amused by Dina's embarrassment. Dina glared at him; how dare he? telling Edna about all of this? Doesn't he know that Edna could deduce that they were once lovers?

The ring of the phone broke the silence. Edna looked at it as if she was waiting for it to stop ringing. After the third ring, Edna picked up the phone and answered. Dina profited to depart from the awkward conversation, but Derrick followed her.

"Wait," said Derrick. "Can I talk to you for a minute?"

"No!" Replied Dina while walking; "I really have to change my clothes and start my job!" she added. At the same time, Edna called Derrick:

"Dr. Lee," said Edna "your mother is on line 1."

"Thank you, Edna," replied Derrick, "I will take it from my office."

Turning to Dina who was already far away from him, he declared "Come with me to say hello to her, she always asks me about you."

"I cannot talk to her right now," answered Dina; "transmit to her my greetings." She added while heading to the cabinet to take her working clothes.

Dina put on her scrubs and went back to Edna who sent her to Doctor Lawrence's office.

"Go to Doctor Lawrence's desk and you will find some patients' charts. Take them and come to place them here alphabetically, then go to the exam rooms to see if everything is in order."

As requested by Edna, Dina headed to Gavin's office to pick up the charts. She knocked at the door, and Doctor Lawrence shouted, "come in". She entered and closed the door behind her.

"Good morning Doctor Lawrence, Edna sent me to pick up some charts," Said Dina, while looking at his desk to see if she could locate the charts.

"Oh yes, the charts... I put them under the desk first layer." Indicated Gavin, while pointing in the direction of the desk layer."

Dina went to grab the charts and thanked Gavin, she opened the door to leave, and encountered Derrick who was coming inside.

"Doctor Lee!" exclaimed Doctor Lawrence joyously, and seeing that Derrick was looking at Dina who was in a hurry to leave the room, Doctor Lawrence said: "Dina, would you stay here for a minute?"

Dina closed the door and stayed inside Doctor Lawrence's office as he requested.

"This is Doctor Derrick Lee, my partner" said Doctor Lawrence to Dina; and addressing Derrick, he said: "Dina had recently graduated as a medical assistant, I just hired her yesterday."

"Well, congratulations Dina, I didn't know that you wanted to be in the medical field," declared Derrick.

Incredulously surprised to hear this statement from Derrick, Dr. Lawrence puckered his eyebrows, looked at them simultaneously and asked:

"Do you two know each other?"

"Yeah, absolutely, we were even engaged, before she decided to move on, but it's a long story, right, Dina?" Said Derrick.

It was the last straw for Dina. Derrick had already ruined the career that she chose once and seems decided to ruin her chance to keep her job in this medical office, and like the first time, she felt that she won't be able to stop him. She wanted to yell that she didn't decided to move on, but was forced to, after he cheated on her.

She opened her mouth, but instead of defending herself, and tell what really happened, she said "I have to go to place those charts, and Edna might need my help at the front office."

"Oh, sure, you can leave now," affirmed Dr. Lawrence, there is no need for further presentation as you two already know each other ...so well." He added

"We definitely know each other well," agreed Derrick.

Dina left immediately. After she finished to place the charts alphabetically, where Edna had asked her to, Dina went to check the exam rooms to see if they were ready for patients to be examined.

Everything was well arranged as she did it the day before. She went to Edna and informed her. Four patients were already in the waiting room.

"You can start to bring patients in the examination rooms to take their vital signs." Mrs. Peterson is the first on our list, you can start with her," said Edna.

Dina took Mrs. Peterson's chart, called her name and accompanied her to the exam room number one, to take her vital signs. Dina wrote the date and the time in the chart log, then, she wrapped the blood pressure cuff of the digital monitor around the upper part of Mrs. Peterson's right arm to take her blood pressure and recorded it on the chart. After that, she asked Mrs. Peterson to open her mouth, and inserted the digital thermometer in, to take her temperature, and recorded it also. Finally, she recorded Mrs. Peterson's respiration rate, as well as her weight on the chart.

"Doctor Lawrence will be with you shortly" she informed Mrs. Peterson, who was six months pregnant and was suffering from high blood pressure.

"Thank you," replied Mrs. Peterson.

Dina put the chart in the pocket located behind the door and went to inform Doctor Lawrence that the patient in room one was ready to be seen. After that, she called the other patients in order of their appointment time.

When it was time to take their break, Edna informed Dina that both she and Dina were expected at the "Office-Resto," a restaurant nearby the office building, to celebrate Dr. Lee's return.

"I'm sorry but I cannot go. I... I brought my lunch," stated Dina.

"It's mandatory for you and me," replied Edna, "order of the Doctors," she added with a big smile.

"I was also counting on calling home," argued Dina.

"Well, you can do it right now before we leave," suggested Edna, while pointing at the office phone.

Dina sat in a chair behind the reception desk and called her parents; she was happy to learn that everything was okay, and that her brother and her parents were reconciled.

"Time to go said Edna, who grabbed her purse, and her sweater; I'm really hungry," she added.

"Go ahead I will rejoin you, I have to get my purse first," replied Dina

"I will wait for you; as weird as it may appear, Doctor Lee asked me to stick to you like a glue until we get to the restaurant."

"Oh, ok" said Dina. She went to pick up her purse and profited to apply a little bit of purple lipstick on her mouth. Then, she followed Edna trough the parking lot.

"Go ahead, I will follow your car," said Dina

"Oh no, let's just take my car, we will be coming back at the office soon," replied Edna. She unlocked her car, and they both went in and left.

Once in front of the restaurant, Edna started looking for a parking space. Realizing that there were none, she decided to park in any available space nearby. While she was passing by, Dina noticed an empty place in the rear of the restaurant; she showed it to Edna, who immediately made a U-turn and took the space.

Chapter 8

As soon as they got inside the restaurant, Doctor Lawrence waved at them. They went to him and sat down. Dina realized that Derrick had not arrived yet. She wanted to ask Doctor Lawrence about him, but she retreated to do so, as she did not want it to be perceived as if she was still interested in him. She opened the menu that was previously disposed in front of her and started looking at it.

Two minutes later, Derrick arrived, and sat on their table.

"I took the liberty to order drinks for everybody, is that okay?" exclaimed Doctor Lawrence

"Sounds good to me" replied Edna. "What did you order for me?"

"I ordered a glass of lemon juice for you," answered Dr. Lawrence, "and a glass of pineapple juice for Dina." He added.

"Thank you," said Edna

"As long as my drink is an orange juice," declared Derrick

"Indeed, I know it is your favorite, that is the one you always order" answered Gavin.

"So, how did you know that Dina would prefer pineapple juice? Asked Derrick, intrigued.

"We simply had a drink last night, and, like me, she chose pineapple juice."

"Oh, I see." "You just hired her yesterday, and you guys are already partying? Very professional," said Derrick ironically.

"Actually, we started partying way before I hired her." Replied Gavin.

"Well, I wish you guys good luck in mixing work and pleasure." Said Derrick.

"Coming from the man who used to mix studies and pleasure, it sounds odd," replied Gavin. "But don't worry, we are still in the friend's zone, so we don't need any luck with that, right Dina?" asked Gavin

"Right," acquiesced Dina, even though she did not really understand what Gavin was implying. "As long as what he said, even gently, had just made Derrick mad as he is right now, I'm okay with it, thought Dina.

"Anyway, thanks for the advice, and welcome back!" added Gavin.

"Welcome back," echoed Edna.

As Dina did not reiterate the *"welcome back"* greeting to Derrick, a complete silence took place. The atmosphere was very tense. Derrick was looking suspiciously at Dina, and Edna was watching the spectacle like she was at the movie theatre. Fortunately, the waiter arrived with their drinks.

"What took you guys so long to serve the drinks today?" Asked Gavin, as the waiter was placing their drinks in front of them. "The last time I came, the service was faster."

"My apologies, I did not notice that your guests had arrived. I will take your food order now if you are ready." Said the server.

They placed their order. Gavin order a buffalo chicken wings with fries, Derrick order the teriyaki salmon with rice, Edna selected the burritos, and Dina ordered a chicken salad. After everyone had finished to place their order, the waiter collected the menus from them.

"Your food will be ready in about twenty minutes," said the server before leaving.

"I really don't see how the food that we order would be ready in twenty minutes," said Dina to break the tense silence.

"Trust me it will. This is "*Office Resto,*" everything is pre-cooked; what they usually do is to reheat the food when people order. Hopefully, we will be able to enjoy our dishes promptly and go back to the office," Answered Gavin.

"My sister is organizing a welcome party for me at my place tonight," informed Derrick. "She assured me that you will be there Gavin, is that right?" He asked Dr. Lawrence; Gavin nodded his head positively. "You guys are welcome to join us." Informed Derrick to Dina and Edna."

"You can count me in," replied Edna; "at what time does it start?" She asked.

"Seven O'clock," disclosed Derrick to Edna. "Can I count you in too Di?" asked Derrick. "I would really appreciate if you could make it."

"Did he really call me Di?" thought Dina, "what does he think he's doing? Doesn't he know that my nickname is exclusively for my family members and my close friends? As far as I recalled, he is none of the above... anymore." Dina wanted to shout it loud to him, but she remembered that her job was on the line. So, she politely declined his invitation.

"Thank you, but I have other plans for tonight." Replied Dina

"Well, I'm very disappointed," said Derrick. "Since I know you, it's the first time that you have refused to come to something that is related to me. You know what it tells me?" Asked Derrick

Since Dina was ignoring his question, Derrick alleged: "You're still in love with me."

Edna who was having a sip of her lemon juice almost chokes.

Dina looked at Gavin, he was looking attentively at her, like him too was waiting for an answer.

"With all due respect, Doctor Lee, I am so over you!" retorted Dina.

"So, prove it, come to my party," maintained Derrick. "And please, call me Derrick as you used to." He added

Momentarily, Dina bowed her head, she felt embarrassed, how could Derrick choose to have this kind of conversation with her in front of her employer and her co-worker?

After a moment, Dina straightened her head and replied:

"There is nothing to prove, Doctor Lee; like I said, I have other plans for tonight."

"Really," sustained Derrick, "would you be kind enough to share these plans with us? Just give me a hint of what you planned to do tonight, besides of taking a shower and sleeping in your bed alone." He joked.

Fortunately, the server arrived with their order. Dina felt relieved from all the awkward conversation.

"Does anybody want more drinks?" asked the server, after placing their respective order of food in front of them. As everyone was shaking their head negatively, the server wished them a "Bon Appetit," and left.

"We are still waiting for some details about your busy program for tonight, Dina." Persisted Derrick

Too ashamed to avow that the only plan she had for tonight were effectively to take a shower and go to bed alone, Dina didn't say anything. Understanding her embarrassment, Gavin came to her rescue.

"Actually, what Dina is reluctant to tell you is that she has a date with me at the Antilleans nightclub tonight." "After that, maybe she will take a shower and go to bed... alone...," added Gavin, amused.

"A date? you two? But Gavin, I thought that you had planned to come to my party tonight?" Asked Derrick promptly.

"I will," assured Gavin. "However, I would have to leave at eight, so I can pick up Dina at her house to finally go to the nightclub." He added, before he took a bite of chicken from his plate and chewed it slowly.

"I see," said Derrick deceived. "But don't you think it would be easier if Dina come to my party at seven, and you two leave together around eight?" He Asked

"I don't know, it's up to Dina," replied Gavin

"Oh, I won't have enough time to prepare myself for my date with Doctor Lawrence if I come to your party." said Dina who immediately picked her fork in her plate and took a bite of lettuce. She placed the lettuce in her mouth and started to chew it automatically.

"I think you would have plenty of time," affirmed Derrick, who had just finish to drink a sip of his juice.

"Not really," insisted Dina "I will finish at the office at five. It will take me about fifteen minutes to get home. Let's not forget that I must eat, take a shower, select my dress, and apply my makeup. You know how girls are when they are going to a date. They really need time to transform themselves in Cinderella for their charming Prince." She explained.

"Specially you, Dina; I remember our first date; we were supposed to go to the theater, but you took so much time preparing yourself, that the place was full when we finally got there. The only seats available were all the way down at the front row. You were so shy that you didn't want to go there. We bought popcorn and soda and went back to our room at the campus to eat. I never forget, it was the first food that we shared together." Said Derrick.

Instantly, Dina lost her appetite. She remembered it was also the same movie theater where she found him with another girl.

Edna and Gavin were eating without making any comments, but Dina knew that they were listening to their conversation.

"He almost fooled me again," thought Dina, "but mentioning the movie theater story brought me back to reality. He's right; I'm still in love with him. I'd better run far away from him to escape his charm."

"You have something green near your lips," said Derrick; he had a white napkin in his right hand and was reaching it towards Dina's face to clean the green stuff.

"Oh no," replied Dina, "I will take care of it."

Dina removed the knife that was still wrapped inside her napkin, took the napkin and wiped around her mouth.

"So, are you coming?" Asked gently Derrick.

It was hard to decline his invitation this time; the way he was asking, the sweet face he was making, the trip he made her make to their past, and the way he was looking at her… all of these made it difficult for Dina to continue to decline his invitation.

"Yes, I will try to make it." Replied Dina

"Well I would really appreciate it. I know behind this hostile face was hiding my sympathetic girl." Joked Derrick

Dina smiled, Derrick always knew how to appease her with his jokes and particularly how to get what he wanted from her. They exchanged their phone number and talk about the fun they had back at the university campus. Now that everybody was conversing with everybody, the atmosphere was more jovial.

After they finished to eat, the server came back to pick up their empty plates, he suggested to them some delicious deserts to taste. Edna chose a cheesecake, but Dina declined, saying that she was on a diet. Derrick and Gavin declined to take a dessert also.

A few minutes after the server brought the cheesecake to Edna, he came back with the bill. Gavin took it and looked at the total; he was about to reach his pocket to take his wallet, but Derrick stopped him, and insisted to pay for their lunch.

"It was so pleasant, that I would feel guilty if I don't pay for it." Said Derrick.

"No way," insisted Gavin, "I organized this lunch to celebrate your return at the office, so the bill is on me."

"As you wish," conceded Derrick.

While Gavin was opening his wallet, Dina seized the occasion to go to the restroom.

"If you'll excuse me, I will be back in a moment", said Dina

Once in the lady's restroom, she touched up her make up, and applied a little bit of lipstick on her mouth. When she came back, Doctor Lawrence and Edna were gone, only Derrick was quietly sitting at their table.

"But where is everybody?" Asked Dina anxiously.

Before answering, Derrick stood up and approached Dina, she backed away instantaneously.

"They went back to the office. Edna wanted to wait for you, but I told her that I will drive you back." He explained.

"Stay away from me, you hear that. I don't know what game you think you're playing with me, but this time, do not expect to win. I'm not getting into your car, and I don't want to be anywhere close to you." Exploded Dina

"Have you finished talking?" Asked Derrick, "It's time for us to go back to the office." He added

"No, you can go alone; I will find a way to get back there all by myself. It's not even twelve hours since I bumped into you and you are already complicating my life. Can't you just leave me alone?" asked Dina with tears coming in her eyes.

"I'm sorry but there's no other way to go back to the office; I didn't know that I was bothering you that much. Just a few minutes ago, before you went to the bathroom, you seemed to enjoy my presence like you used to. I just wanted to be alone with you to ask for your forgiveness, but now I know that I don't have any chance to get you back. I promise if you let me drive you back, it will be the last time that I will cause you any inconvenience; I will leave you alone. But for now, I'm afraid that you are stuck with me here." Explained Derrick

"Okay," agreed Dina, as she realized that she did not have any other choice.

Dina was cracking her knuckles, and her lips were involuntary compressing together. Derrick figured out that Dina was still nervous around him; he slightly touched her hands and said:

"Relax Dina, it's me, you know you don't have anything to be afraid of, I promise that I won't try to kiss you, even though I'm really tempted to do so," he added.

"I'm not scared of you; it's just too much for me to bear in one day; and let me remind you that you're not good at keeping your promises." Replied Dina.

"Yes, I did, I kept my promise to you." Said Derrick

"No, you didn't, you were seeing someone else behind my back Derrick." Argued Dina

"But I never left you, you left me. My promise was to never leave you, and I kept it. You are the one that didn't keep your promise. You left me without even try to save our love. If it was me, I would never abandon you without a fight, I would try to save our love before running away like you did." Reproached Derrick

"I cannot believe that you are blaming me for your infidelity." Retorted Dina

"I'm blaming you for deserting me, not for my infidelity. Now that I know I cannot live without you, I'm willing to change. I just wish that I didn't hurt you that hard before realizing that," Derrick said gloomily.

This tone Dina knew it, and it was the tone that Derrick used when he was sad, or frustrated. Dina felt sorry for him, she just wanted to take him in her arms and comfort him, but she restrained herself to do so.

"You are right, I shouldn't have left you without a fight," admitted Dina. "I'm really sorry, I thought you didn't care," she added

"I do care. I never stopped loving you Dina," said Derrick.

"Look, until now, I never realized that I was also responsible for our breakup, but the only thing I always knew is that I will never trust you again. Will we get back together? I don't know about that. It sounds weird to me to just start talking about love with you. I think it would be better if we tried to simply be friends. Now, let's just go back to the office." Suggested Dina

Derrick acquiesced, and they walked silently to the restaurant exit door.

From his office, Gavin was looking at the staff parking space; Derrick's space was empty. It was going to be two o'clock in five minutes, and Edna had already reopened the office door. Where are they? Wondered Gavin. "I should have never left Dina alone with Derrick," he thought. They were reconciled, he was witness of it, and he knew they could be anywhere celebrating their reconciliation. He was afraid that Dina and Derrick were having some sort of "*Former Lovers Reunion*," Dina's favorite show.

Chapter 9

After they left the restaurant, Derrick guided Dina to the street corner where he had left his car. He opened the front passenger door ceremonially for her. She thanked him and sat down. Then, he closed the door, and went to sit behind the wheel.

While he was driving, he turned quickly to Dina and said:

"Can I ask you a question, as a friend?"

"Sure," replied Dina, curious

"You seem to be really closed to Gavin, how did you two meet?"

"One night, I went to the Antillean nightclub with some friends and he invited me to dance, this is how we met." Explained Dina

"*You,* Dina, *you* went to a nightclub with friends? I cannot believe that. Do you remember that I had to practically drag you to go in this kind of place with me?" Asked Derrick

"Yeah, and we would dance all night long," said Dina nostalgically.

"It seems to be a routine for you now," alleged Derrick

"What makes you think that?" Asked Dina.

"Well, you are going to the nightclub with Gavin tonight, again," maintained Derrick.

"Right, I guess now I'm addicted to the nightclub like I was addicted to you." Mocked Dina.

"I really hope that your addiction is to the nightclub, not to Gavin," replied Derrick.

"And what if I'm addicted to both: Gavin and the nightclub?" Asked Dina defiantly.

"In that case I would have to warn you: he's a womanizer, he will break your heart." Alleged Derrick

"Thanks for the advice; I will keep it in mind each time I will be on a date with him." Replied Dina.

"So, you are continuing to date him?" Asked Derrick.

"You bet, I really don't see why I shouldn't", argued Dina.

"I just told you, the man is a seducer," persisted Derrick.

"Well, obviously you didn't convince me Derrick," maintained Dina.

"Maybe you will be convinced after you have slept with him and then he dumps you." Insisted Derrick

"Just like you did, right? I slept with you and you dumped me for another girl," declared Dina

"You and I had a different relationship Dina, we were engaged." Argued Derrick

"How does the fact that we were engaged make our relationship different, Derrick? My parents didn't know anything about it. The only difference is that now because of you, I know what men are capable of, and I'm more armed to defend myself against their ruse." Replied Dina insolently, while pointing her index finger at him.

"Calm down Dina, I was just giving you an advice." Replied Derrick.

"Maybe you had better give me this advice about yourself two years ago. What about you save it for the next girl who will have the misfortune to fall in love with you?" Suggested Dina

"Look, I'm really sorry that I hurt you Dina. Trust me, I never meant to. I just hope that you will forgive me because like I told you just a few minutes ago, I'm still in love with you." Declared Derrick

"Really? If you think that coming to me all sweet and telling me that you are still in love with me is going to keep me away from Doctor Lawrence, you are wasting your time Derrick Lee!" Warned Dina.

"The fact that I'm still in love with you has nothing to do with Gavin," replied Derrick, "but yes, it really bothers me to know that you are dating him." He added.

"I wouldn't call it "*dating*," but I will continue to go out with Doctor Lawrence, whether you like it or not! I will do whatever pleases me with him even if it bothers you! You're the one that was unfaithful, why should you get something to say about who I should go out with or not?" Asked Dina

"Going out with him or dating him are the same. I just hope that you are not going to regret it every day of your life as I did in the last two years. Because when you are aware that you are making a mistake as it was in my case, but you persist on doing it, trust me, the worse is not being able to forgive yourself." Said Derrick

"Well, I guess that it won't hurt me to make a "mistake" deliberately, as dating you was a big one that I made ingenuously." Replied Dina.

"Dina please, do not punish yourself because of me. Run as far as you can from Gavin, he's not the kind of guy that would ever marry you." Alleged Derrick

"You weren't the kind of guy that would marry me either Derrick, remember? Maybe he's not going to marry me, but at least he didn't betray me yet. He gets something that you will never have: my trust, and there is nothing that you can say about him that would obliterate that." Replied Dina.

"Gavin was still wondering about Dina and Derrick, and observing the vacant parking space, when Derrick arrived and parked. He saw Dina getting out of the car and slammed the door. She looked very upset. Gavin's heartbeat accelerates, and he felt relieved to see her back to the office. "It's been a long time that I ever had this feeling for someone; oh no! I'm in love with Dina…" realized Gavin.

Dina felt a tremendous relief that they had finally arrived at the office. As soon as Derrick parked, she jumped out of the car.

"It was nice talking to you. See you later." Shouted Derrick as Dina was walking towards the entry of the office.

Dina did not answer, she went straight to the bathroom, washed her hands, and went to call the next patient. After taking the patient chief of complaint, she closed the door halfway behind her, and went to inform Doctor Lawrence.

"Mrs. Chavez is ready to be seen," said Dina to Gavin. "She's in room two."

"Room two? Why isn't she in room one?" Asked Gavin.

"Doctor Lee is examining Mrs. Williams in room one." Answered Dina

"Did you already take her vital signs?" Asked Gavin

"No, but I think that Edna did, because her chart was in the pocket of room one when I came from lunch. I looked at it and her vital signs were recorded in today's date." Explained Dina

"Well thank you, I will be there in a few minutes." Said Gavin.

Gavin wanted to ask Dina why she and Derrick took so long to return to the office, and why she was so upset when they arrived at the parking lot; but he refrained to do so. "It's a personal matter; I don't want her to think that I'm interested in her private life. She might guess that I'm in love with her, and that's the last thing I want her to know." Thought Gavin.

Gavin washed his hands and wiped them. Then, he took his stethoscope place it around his neck. After that, He got out of his office, and locked the door. He knocked at the door of room number two that was halfway open and entered. Mrs. Chavez was sitting on a chair, Gavin greeted her, and asked her about her newborn baby that he had personally delivered by C-section. Then, he closed the door behind himself, and Dina could not hear anything anymore.

Dina had just finished accompanying Mrs. Cooper in room number tree, when Gavin called her, and ask her to bring two samples of vaginal rinse for Mrs. Alvarez. She went into the supplies area and came back with two little bottles and gave them to Mrs. Alvarez.

"Use it twice a day, and if you're satisfied with the result, you can buy more over the counter at any drugstore." Explained dr. Lawrence.

Dina went back to room three and took Mrs. Cooper's vital sign. Then, she went to Doctor Lawrence and notified him that Mrs. Cooper was ready to be seen.

"I think that I'm going to let Dr. Lee take care of her. I need you to go to the front office, find those patients phone numbers from their chart, and call each of them to remind them of their appointment tomorrow, said Gavin, while handing to Dina the list with the patients' date of birth."

"Before you call them, be sure their birthday matches their social security numbers that you will find in their charts; we have a few patients that have the same first and last names." Said Gavin.

Dina went to the front desk and notified Edna that Dr. Lee would be the one to examine Mrs. Cooper. Then, as instructed by Doctor Lawrence, she took the list and searched for the patients' phone numbers from their chart and called them to remind them of their appointment at the office the next day.

It was almost five thirty in the evening when Dina finally left the office. She had to stay to clean up the examination rooms, change the exam table papers, and add more band-aid, spatulas, and gloves to the rooms. Edna had already left, as she was so excited to go to prepare herself to go to Derrick's party. Dina was already in the parking lot when she remembered that she forgot to tell Doctor Lawrence that she was leaving. She went back and knocked at his door.

"Come in," answered Gavin

Dina pushed the door and entered inside Gavin's office.

"I just remember that I forgot to tell you that I was leaving." Said Dina

"Oh, it's five O'clock already?" asked Doctor Lawrence

"Actually, it's almost five fifteen. I was setting the exam rooms in order before leaving; I just finished

"Well, thank you for your extra time. How was your little trip with Doctor Lee?" asked Gavin

"It was quite enjoyable," lied Dina

"Good, so you're… still coming to his party tonight, right?" asked Gavin

"Right," answered Dina, embarrassed

"Well, see you later then. I hope you will be ready on time for once," joked Gavin

"I will try my best," replied Dina

While passing near Derrick's office, Dina heard him talking on the phone. "He's still here," thought Dina. "Maybe I should say goodbye to him… No, he will think that I'm trying to get close to him," assumed Dina. She continued to walk and exited the office.

After she got into her car, Dina opened her handbag, and took a lipstick; she opened it, and applied a little bit on her dry mouth. She had the sensation that someone was watching her, so she instinctively looked at the office window and saw Gavin observing her. She smiled, and waved at him, put on her seatbelt, and left the parking lot.

Derrick was standing behind his window, and saw Dina cheerfully weaving while looking at Gavin's window. "I think it's time for me to talk man to man to Gavin." Resolved Derrick.

Immediately, he left his office, and went to Gavin's.

"Can I talk to you, in private," Asked Derrick.

"Sure, there's only you and I here right now, Dina and Edna had already left. Is everything alright?" Asked Gavin, as he saw Derrick looking very serious.

"Yeah, I just wanted to talk to you about Dina," replied Derrick

"Dina, what about her?" Asked Gavin, intrigued

"Remember, I told you that we were dating back at the university?" Asked Derrick

"Right, but isn't it the past now? You two are not together anymore Derrick." Argued Gavin

"I'm just asking you politely to back-off. Don't you see she's still in love with me?" Said Derrick

"Good for you Derrick, but it is with me that she's going on a date after your party tonight." Stated Gavin

"There's nothing between you two as you seem to insinuate Gavin, she's still calling you Doctor Lawrence." Insisted Derrick

"She's still calling you Doctor Lee; does that means that you two weren't dating?" Argued Gavin

"I don't believe you. She's not interested in any one else than me." maintained Derrick

"Derrick, Derrick, Derrick," said Gavin while shaking his head, I think you really need a reality check. When was the last time that you saw her before you two jumped into each other here in this medical office? Let me guess: almost three years, right?" Asked Gavin

"Right, but what is your point?" Asked Derrick, irritated.

"I mean, did she ever go back to see you? Better yet, did she ever call you? No, never! She's trying to heal from a broken heart. She might not be completely over you but, believe me she's no longer in love with you. As any betrayed woman, she's trying to see if her charm still works on you. It's not called love Derrick; she's just trying to get her confidence back." Replied Gavin.

"That's not true, you don't know what you are talking about Gavin," argued Derrick

"You know I'm right Derrick, deep inside your heart you know she's planning something against you, it's called revenge." Said Gavin

"You are just speculating, Gavin; there is no reason for her to plan whatever you think she intend to do to me." Replied Derrick

"No reason?! You cheated on her Derrick, and by dating someone else behind her back, you had attacked her pride and her confidence. Now that she found an occasion, she's going to shake your world to take back everything you stole from her when you duped her. Once she's done with you, I guarantee you that you will be the one trying to seduce her to get her back, but she will never give you another chance." Explained Gavin

"Well, tonight you might be surprised; I think she's going to give me another chance sooner than I expected," bragged Derrick

"If it's true, I wouldn't call it chance if I were you. Dina is insecure around men, she's uncomfortable particularly around men of our race because of what you did to her. She really thinks that all of us are like you. You are her therapy; her subconscious is dictating her to get her remedies from you, who are the source of her lack of confidence. She is using you to regain what you took from her: her dignity; after that, she will break your heart as you had broken hers. That all she's doing and from what I see, you are getting right into her web Derrick." Said Gavin

"I think it's my turn to thank you for your advice. But I still maintain my position: back the fuck off. You are the one trying to get her into your web, but for what? Just to make your pathetic family humiliate her. The last woman you had did not have the approval of your parents because she didn't come from a rich family like yours, even though she's from our race; do you think your family will ever accept Dina with her dark complexion and her nappy hair? Asked Derrick

As Gavin did not answer, Derrick added:

"That's what I thought. If you really love her, you would let her be happy with me, and protect her from the cruelty of your family. I know what your dad is capable of just to keep her away from you. Now tell me, which one of us really needed a reality check?" Asked Derrick

"You are so worried that I would steal Dina from you, Derrick, but in your place, I would be more worried of the fate that she reserved to you for dumping her." Said Gavin finally.

"I will marry Dina, Gavin, and one day you will be the one worried about what I could do to her. But for now, I'm more preoccupied on getting you out of our hair." Replied Derrick, he walked out of Gavin's office and slammed the door behind him.

Chapter 10

A t 6:30 p.m., Dina had already finished to prepare herself.

"Are you going somewhere?" Asked her father when she went to the living room.

"Yes, one of the Doctors is having a party, and all the staff is invited." Replied Dina

"You do know that I need the car to go to work tonight, right?" Said Dina's father

"Right, one of the staff members is coming to pick me up before seven o'clock." Explained Dina

"Oh, okay. Is that a man or a woman?" Dina's father asked immediately

"What difference does it makes?" Replied Dina's mother

"A big one: a woman would give her a ride mostly because she would want to befriend her as a coworker. However, a man would do it just to seduce the new employee that she is." Explained her father

"You and your odd supposition!" Joked Dina's mother

"That's just common sense. A man who's not interested will not bother to pick up a woman he just met at work. Sounds like a date to me." Said Dina's father

"Stop speculating" Said Dina's mother. "Dina didn't say that the person is a man." She argued

"Well, let's just ask her." Proposed her father

As Dina was looking at the clock, pretending that she didn't hear, her father yelled:

"Dina, is the person giving you the ride a guy, or a woman?"

"It's a guy," avowed Dina embarrassed.

"That's what I thought." Teased her father

The entrance door rang, and Dina's father went to open. It was Dr. Lawrence. Dina's father invited him to enter. Doctor Lawrence introduced himself to Dina's family:

"I'm Gavin Lawrence, it's a pleasure to meet you Mr. and Mrs. Joseph. We are very blessed to have your daughter working with us at the office," Said Gavin

Gavin was sitting in the living room, and Dina's father asked him since when he started working at the office.

"I started working there three years ago, while I was still in medical school, it was my father's medical office at that time. Now, I co-own it with an old friend of mine, Doctor Derrick Lee." Explained Gavin.

"That is very wise of you to follow your father's footsteps; he has someone to pass the torch to. He must be really proud of you." Said Dina's father

"I suppose he is, anyway he's retired now, and at least I inherited his patients and his office." Explained Gavin

"What about your associate, is his father a Doctor also?" Enquired Dina's father

Dina stood up immediately, look at her watch and said: "It's almost seven o'clock, we should leave now."

"Why the sudden rush?" asked her father. "I just ask about your employer's associate and you immediately stood up to leave." He added

"We were supposed to be there at seven, dad; it's five minutes before seven now, we are going to be late." Said Dina.

"It's just a party Dina, people can show up anytime in between. Now tell me about your other boss." Pressed her father

"Not now dad, please..." Begged Dina

"Is there anything about this man that we should know?" Persisted her father

"We really have to go dad." Replied Dina

"Well, I'm sorry, but you cannot leave until you tell me what is going on. It's like I pressed on a sensitive button when I asked about your other boss. Just tell me what the matter is with him." Urged her father

"I can't, not now dad, don't do that to me please," begged Dina

"In this case, I don't have any other choice than making you stay, Dina. I hope you understand," stated her father

"May I say something?" asked Gavin.

"Go ahead," acquiesced Dina's father.

"I believe Dina would be more comfortable to talk to you about this matter in private, you know, when there's no stranger around." Indicated Gavin while pointing at himself.

Gavin sounded so funny that Dina's mother couldn't help but laugh. But her father was not in the mood for jokes, "I agree with you," he replied to Gavin. Then, he turned towards Dina and said:

"I will be waiting for you tonight, so we can talk about it. At what time should I expect you?"

"Probably around eleven," lied Dina. She wanted to postpone the time that she had to explain her past relationship to Derrick.

"We will continue this conversation at eleven then." Agreed her father

"But honey, you forget that you have to go to work tonight." Reminded Dina's mother

"I completely forgot. Well, I guess we will have to wait for tomorrow to address this matter. You may go now young lady." Said her father.

Dina acquiesced. She was happy that the discussion with her dad was over for now. She stood up, and headed towards the exit door, followed by Gavin.

"It was nice meeting you, Mr. and Mrs. Joseph," said Gavin

"Likewise, Doctor Lawrence," replied her father.

"It was a pleasure meeting you too," replied her mother

Gavin opened the passenger door for Dina, she sat there, and he closed the door and went to the driver side to go behind the wheel. As Gavin was turning the ignition key on, Julie approach the car to talk to Dina.

"Dina, are you going somewhere?" And, looking at the driver side, she added: "you have a date? finally!"

"Julie? you scared me!" exclaimed Dina, "what are you doing here?" asked Dina

"You still didn't tell me the story, you remember? the one with your new employer, it looks like it's the same car as the other night." Replied Julie

"I said during the week-end, Julie, remember? I have to go now, we are going to be late." Said Dina

"Not before introducing me to your date," replied Julie, while walking towards the driver's side.

"Hi, I'm Julie Sullivan, Dina's neighbor and childhood friend." Said Julie

"Gavin Lawrence," replied Gavin, "nice to meet you Julie."

"Your face looks familiar," observed Julie. "Do I know you from somewhere?" She asked

"It must be from the nightclub, the other night," replied Gavin

"Yes! I knew I have seen you before! I'm glad that you two made up with each other. It's seems like something was really clicking between you two the night that you were dancing together." Said Julie, and turning to Dina, she added:

"You did not have to lie, telling me that he was your boss the other night, Dina, I would have understood you know."

"I was not lying to you Julie, Doctor Lawrence is my employer, and we are going to his associate's welcome party... first," replied Dina

"I knew it, I knew it was also a date. You were never a good liar Dina. So where are you guys going after the party?" asked Julie

"I don't mean to be rude, but we must go now, announced Gavin while starting the car. It was a pleasure meeting you Julie," Gavin added, before leaving. Dina waved at Julie from the rearview of the car.

"Your neighbor is a piece of work," said Gavin. "She could be a brilliant detective if she ever wanted to be one."

"Tell me about it," replied Dina; "I didn't even see her coming, she knows most of the things that is happening in my house without us telling her anything. But she is a good friend though, nobody's perfect right?"

"Yeah, I guess you are right," replied Gavin, "nobody's perfect."

After Dina and Gavin left, Dina's mother sat near her husband on the couch and asked:

"How did you know that the person that was giving Dina the ride was a guy?"

"Didn't you see how Dina was dressed? Her outfits perfectly harmonize elegance and seduction; I know something was going on. I planned to go to the bottom of this. Doctor Lawrence seems to be a nice and respectful young man, but his associate must be either a mean guy full of prejudice or a seducer. I won't be surprise if he is both, but definitely he's not treating our daughter as he should at the office." Explained Dina's father

"That's just an assumption honey, I admit that something might be wrong with her other boss, but I'm sure it has nothing to do with Dina." Said Dina's mother

"I hope you're right, but the way that I saw Dina reacted when I asked about that guy make me think that it surely has something to do with her." Deduced Dina's father.

"She's so happy to have this job, I don't want to see you keeping her from going to work there just because one of her bosses has any weird behavior towards her, should he be full of prejudice or a seducer." Warned Dina's mother

"As long as she lives under my roof, I will make sure that she doesn't stay in any places where she is being harassed, or where her integrity is compromised; even if it's a workplace or a school establishment, it doesn't matter. Her well-being is all that matters." Argued Dina's father

"I completely agree with you but promise me that you won't ask her to leave her job." Requested her mother.

"I'm sorry but I can't guarantee you that. I need to know the facts before I could make such a promise to you." Contested her father

"I understand but I just don't want you to punish her because of someone else's behavior. If we ever found out that this guy's conduct at work is unacceptable, making Dina quit her job would be like punishing her for his conduct, and it will not be fair to her." Maintained Dina's mother

Dina's father looked at the large green clock in the hall and stated:

"It is 7:30 already, I have to go to prepare myself to go to work. We will resume this discussion when everybody will be at home."

Immediately, Dina's father went to take a shower, and left for work.

Chapter 11

When Gavin and Dina arrived at Derrick's party, it was already packed with people.

"Oh, I didn't know there will be so much people, it seems like Derrick has invited the whole town." Gavin shouted to Dina.

"I thought it would be his family members and close friends only," replied Dina

"I'm going to get something to drink, what can I bring for you", asked Gavin

"Anything that does not contain alcohol," said Dina

"Wise choice," joked Gavin, before he went to get the drinks

Dina was looking at Gavin's who was trying to find a way through the crowd to go to the bar, when Derrick arrived from nowhere.

"I'm glad that you could make it Dina, can I offer you a drink," Derrick asked

"Don't bother, Gavin just went to get me one, you have a lot of guests to take care of, but thanks for offering." Replied Dina

"He did, didn't he, but hopefully the night is still young; I'm sure I will get my turn to get you something." Declared Derrick

"If I were you, I wouldn't be so sure; Gavin and I will leave at eight." Said Dina

"We still have more than forty minutes; it's less than the amount of time that I need to win you back." Asserted Derrick

Dina could not hold her laugh,

"You're joking, right" asked Dina

"No, I'm serious. I really hope that tonight will be the night that you will finally decide to give me a second chance." Said Derrick

Dina did not have time to answer to Derrick, as Gavin had arrived and handed her a bottle of beer.

"Are you trying to get me drunk? Asked Dina to Gavin, "it's a beer that you brought me, have you not realized that? She added amused.

"My bad answered Derrick, I only order alcoholic beverages as all my guests are adults."

Immediately, Dina became serious. She was trying to understand why Derrick would only serve alcoholic beverages at his party. Without further consideration, she decided to discuss the matter with him.

"Isn't it imprudent to only serve alcoholic beverages? Did you forget that most of your guests get to drive themselves home?" Asked Dina

"Fortunately for you, Gavin is the one driving; I suppose you will be safe with him." Replied Derrick

"I can assure you that she will," responded Gavin

"How can you be so sure?" Argued Derrick

"I'm drinking with moderation, that's the most important precaution to take." Retorted Gavin

"I think the most suitable precaution for you to take is to go home alone directly after the party, and I will drop Dina at her house." Proposed Derrick

"Here we go again!" exclaimed Gavin. "Look Derrick, if you want to ask Dina out, go ahead; just take your chance and ask her; but please, stop being mad at me because she and I are going on a date tonight."

"I'm not mad at you, I just want Dina to go back home safely, that's why I'm offering to accompany her." Claimed Derrick

"Well, too bad, I personally pick her up at her house; I have the responsibility to bring her back to her parents'." Explained Gavin

"Can I?" asked Dina, who grabbed the bottle of beer from Gavin and drank a sip of it.

Then, she wiped her mouth and said: "why don't you let me do the drinking, so you can be the sober one, Gavin? If you let me have your drink too, it will be at your own advantage you know. I heard that taking advantages of unconscious drunk women is the most typical for men."

"Well, I guess I'm not your average man," replied Gavin. "I prefer a fully awake and lucid woman," he added, while grabbing back the bottle of beer from her hand.

"Fine," replied Dina, "keep your beer; I'm sure Derrick would not mind guiding me where I can find another one."

"With pleasure," replied Derrick. He grabbed Dina's hand and guided her through the corner of the large dining room transformed in bar station. Dina turned her head to look at Gavin, he gave her a cold stare look.

At 8 p.m., Gavin came to Dina, who was talking to Edna. He found her with another bottle of beer. Dina was so drunk that she had to lean against the wall to keep her balance. When Gavin tried to take the bottle of beer away from Dina, she resisted, arguing that she was still thirsty.

"In this case, you should be drinking water, not beer," replied firmly Gavin, while escorting her in an isolated area of the room.

"No, I don't want any water. Beer contains water, and guess what? it makes me feel sexy; Derrick just told me how attractive I am when I'm drunk," argued Dina

"Tell me why I'm not surprised! what he meant is how much vulnerable you are right now, trust me," alleged Gavin

"If vulnerable means having a man to hold me tonight, I'm fine with it. Do you know when the last time a man held me in his arms?" Asked Dina

"It's not the place to talk about that," replied Gavin; "come on let's go," he added.

"Where are we going?" Asked Dina. As Gavin did not answer, she continued: "the only place I want to go right now is your house. Do you have a big bed in your room? I love big beds."

Derrick was talking with his sister and her fiancé when he saw Gavin attempting to take a bottle of beer away from Dina. He excused himself, slink away, and went to see what was going on

"Please stop talking Dina." Begged Gavin, just follow me

"Just follow you, wow! Since you don't want her to talk, I'd like to know where you planned on taking her," inquired Derrick

"Derrick, please, stay out of this," warned Gavin; "come on Dina let's go" added Gavin

"No, stay with me Dina," replied Derrick, "I will drop you to your house right after the party."

"I want to go with Gavin, I don't want to go to bed alone tonight."

"You are drunk, Dina, you don't know what you are saying. Stay with me and you won't be alone; you know I'm the one that you can trust here," maintained Derrick

"I don't want to stay with you Derrick, don't you see? You are the one that broke my heart. The only person I can trust here is Gavin, and he's the one that I should follow." Replied Dina

"If you go with Gavin, you will make the same mistake that you did with me; but if you stay with me, I promise that I will make things right between us; I will marry you. I am ready to propose to you in front of everybody here tonight if you want me to, and they will be witness of my promise. All I'm asking you is to give our love a second chance. It's your choice now," he added while extending his right arm towards her and opening his hand.

Dina could not resist, it was a dream come true for her. For a moment, she remembered how many times she had dreamed of Derrick asking her, once again, to marry him. She started walking towards him, but once half way, she turned around, and looked at Gavin; he looked surprise and sad at the same time. Dina couldn't go any step further. She bowed her head, crossed her harms over her chest, and ran towards the exit door. Gavin went after her and caught her outside.

"I'm ready to go," said Dina to Gavin

"Me too," replied Gavin, "let's get out of here."

Dina was so drunk that she was slipping up, Gavin offered his right arm to her, she passed her left hand on it, and they walked silently towards his car. Once inside the car, Dina started shaking.

70

"Are you ok?" Asked Gavin

"Yeah, it's kind of cold here," complained Dina.

Gavin took his jacket off and put it on Dina's shoulder. "This will keep you warm, let me pass the heat for you also."

"I didn't realize it was going to be so cold tonight." Said Dina

"Well, it's not summer anymore, fall had started; the temperature often drops like that at night." Replied Gavin

Gavin put his seatbelt, and asked Dina to do the same. "Where are we going" asked Dina, after she finished to put her seat belt.

"I'm dropping you off at your house." Replied Gavin

"What about the nightclub?" asked Dina

"You are way too intoxicated to go there; maybe another time," explained Gavin

"No, I'm not that intoxicated, let's go dancing!" Argued Dina

"The only place you should go tonight is your bed; therefore, I'm driving you to your house, so you can have a good night's sleep." Said Gavin

"Oh no! not in my house! my mother is surely awake; she might smell the odor of alcohol on me", pleaded Dina.

"It's not the first time that you've been drunk at night, Dina. I wonder where your parents were the night that I encountered you, you were also drunk, do you remember?" Said Gavin

"It was the first time…" argued Dina.

"Sure, it was…" replied Gavin skeptically. "I bet your parents are going to think tonight is also the first time that you have been drunk, right?" Persisted Gavin

"Please don't bring me back home like that," begged Dina, "just let me stay in your car; I will leave after I clear my head."

"It's way too chilly outside, you cannot stay in the car; you could get sick." Said Gavin

"Let me stay at your house then, I would sit on a chair until I feel better." Suggested Dina

"I noticed that your vital body functions are starting to decrease. It will take some time for your body to metabolize the alcohol, Dina." Explained Gavin

"Well I will stay as long as it will take me to sober up." Replied Dina

"What about your parents, they would be worried about you Dina." Said Gavin

"I can call home, and tell my mother that your car broke down or something…" Responded Dina

Gavin looked at her with a surprised expression on his face.

"What? With all due respect Doctor Lawrence, don't tell me that you never lied even once in your entire life." Said Dina

"I'm not judging you, you know, I'm just curious to know what would happen if your parents knew that you were at my house." Said Gavin

"They would freak out, thinking that I'm messing up the only chance that I have to find a decent husband" Explained Dina

"Wow, in this case let me borrow you my phone to call them and tell them your fake story about my car being broken down," said Gavin while taking his phone from his windshield mount. Dina took the phone from Gavin and tried in vain to dial her parents' number.

"Do you even remember the number?" Asked Gavin

"Yes, I'm just too dozy to dial it; I can't even feel my fingers." Said Dina

"Just give me the phone number and I will dial it for you," proposed Gavin, who pulled into a nearby parking lot, and removed the phone from her.

"The number is 317…" Started Dina

"317…" repeated Gavin; but Dina had already passed out.

Gavin started the car, turned around, and drove towards his house. Once he arrived, he opened his garage door, and parked the car inside. Dina was still sleeping. Gavin did not wake her up; instead, he stayed with her inside the car all night long.

It was already five o'clock in the morning when Dina woke up. She turned around, and saw that Gavin was sleeping in the driver seat near her. "How did I end up here?" She wondered. I really messed up this time, I might lose my job and my parents might throw me out of the house. She quietly unbuckled her seatbelt, opened the door of the car to get out, but the door creaked and woke up Gavin.

"Are you feeling okay," he asked

"Yeah, I must go home now," said Dina

"Sure, I will drive you, you sure you don't want to take a shower first?" asked Gavin

"No, I'm good, I just want to go home," affirmed Dina

"Okay, adjust your seatbelt then." Instructed Gavin

He was driving a mile away already, when he realized that Dina would not talk.

"Are you always that quiet in the morning?" Asked Gavin

"I'm sorry I... I have something else in my mind," replied Dina

"You worried about your parents' reactions, right?" asked Gavin

"Yep, I have deceived them once again," said Dina

"Don't be so hard on yourself, you were just enjoying a night out," replied Gavin

"Yeah, I suppose I was; now, I might have to face the consequences," assumed Dina

"Don't be so dramatic Dina, it must not be that bad, you are a twenty-five years old woman." Argued Gavin

"Not in my house, I'm still considered as if I were a child at home, and I kind of like it. Knowing that I disappointed them make me feel ashamed." Explained Dina

When Gavin parked the car, Dina's mother went to them outside on her nightdress.

"Where were you Dina?" Asked her mother. "I passed the night awake, waiting for you." She added

"I was... I was..." repeated Dina

"She was with me, Mrs. Joseph," replied Gavin. One of my patients had an emergency, and it appears that she doesn't like the long time waiting of emergency room. I had to go to visit her at her house to provide care for her, right away. Dina was assisting me. I'm sorry, I kept her so busy that she was unable to call you and let you know.

"Oh, in this case, it's okay. I'm glad that she helped; how is your patient doing? Is she okay now?" Inquired Dina's mother

"Yes, she said that she felt way better now, I'll be seeing her at my office early on Monday for a follow up, right Dina?" Asked Gavin

"Yes," responded Dina

"But isn't emergency room better equipped to provide care in case of emergency? asked Dina's mother

"You are right about that Mrs. Joseph, but it depends of which kind of emergency; this patient urgent situation, fortunately was not too critical," he added, while glancing at Dina. "Luckily, my professional care was enough for her last night, I hope she will continue to follow my instructions to avoid this… kind of situation." Explained Gavin

"Oh, I see, and what was your patient's emergency again?" Asked Dina's mother, suspicious.

"Unfortunately, Mrs. Joseph I cannot disclose this information to you because of the patient's confidentiality. I'm forbidden by law to discuss my patients' condition without their consent." replied Gavin

"Oh, okay, I understand. Well, you must be very exhausted by now, I'm not going to hold you more. Thank you for taking the time to bring Dina home." Said Dina's mother

"It was a pleasure to me to have her by my side during this whole event," replied Gavin.

Gavin shakes hands with Dina and her mother and left. Dina's mother closed the entrance door and declared:

"I'm going to try to sleep now, and I would advise you to do the same." Dina took her mother's advice, went to her room, brushed her teeth and went to bed immediately.

Chapter 12

A few hours later, it was already Saturday. Dina woke up around 10:00 am; her parents and her brother were still sleeping. She realized that she didn't even know when her father came from work. She felt tired, and anxious; it must be the effects of drinking she taught. She prepared herself and decided to go for a walk; "walking might improve my mood, and while walking, I can check in some open stores for a part-time job to add to my current job." She has plans for her future, and this medical assistant job alone will not allow her to accomplish them.

Dina walked a few blocks away from her neighborhood; she was feeling good already. her energy was back, and she felt relaxed. she entered in a coffee shop, and one of the employees asked her what she wanted to order.

"Are you hiring?" asked Dina

"I'm not sure, but I can give you an application that you can fill out. The manager will contact you if we need someone." Replied the employee

"Thank you," said Dina who stood in a corner, to fill out the application.

"Good morning sir, what would you like to order today?" Asked the employee

"I will take a medium caramel mocha and a muffin, please." Answered the customer

"Would you like to try one of our delicious donuts?" continued the employee

"No, thank you, I will stick to my order today". replied Gavin.

"Ok," agreed the employee." The total is seven dollars and fifty cents."

Gavin took he's card from his wallet and slid it in the machine. After putting his card back in his wallet, Gavin went to the other line that says pick-up, to wait for his order. While standing there, he saw Dina standing at the right corner of the store writing something on a paper. He approached her and looked over her shoulder; he discovered that she was filling out a job application.

"Are you searching for a new job?" Asked Gavin. "Are you planning on leaving the office?"

Dina startled, she did not see Gavin coming…

"No, I… just need an extra job; if I could find one part time, it would be perfect. My brother and I are planning to move to our own place. We feel like we are getting too much from our parents without giving them anything; it's time for us to fly with our own wings." Said Dina

"Oh, I see, you guys want to be independent?" Enquired Gavin

"Right, but my brother does not have a steady job; so, I have to find a part-time job to add to my current employ if I want us to be qualified for an apartment lease." Explained Dina

"There's no need for that, I can co-sign the lease for you," proposed Doctor. Lawrence.

"You will do that?" Asked Dina, surprised

"Sure, you are my employee, I don't want you to work too jobs and be so tired that my business would suffer.

"I understand," replied Dina. "Well, I should go now; today is Saturday and it is my turn to cook at home."

"By the way, how is everything at home? Your mother is a very tough woman, she was asking me a lot of questions, and seemed to be suspicious of our story." Enquired Gavin

"Everything is okay presently, but if you think that my mother is tough, wait until you get scrutinized by my dad." Responded Dina

"Oh, I can tell that your father is tough too, I witnessed how much he was pressing you to answer his questions about Derrick. Now, I understand why you didn't want your parents to know the truth about last night." Said Gavin

Dina felt embarrassed as soon as he mentioned last night event. Why did she have to get drunk again and put herself in display in front of Derrick's friends. The worst of all was having to ask Gavin to lie to her mother about the reason why she did not come home last night.

"I really must go now, it's almost time to start cooking," claimed Dina nervously.

"Ok, see you on Monday then." Said Gavin

Once at home, Dina placed a cup of dry black bean in a medium pot, poured two cups of cold water in it and placed the pot on the stove; After that, she turned the burner underneath it to medium and covered the pot with the lid to boil. Then, she took the chicken from the refrigerator, cleaned it with lemon and white vinegar, and rinsed the chicken.

Finally, Dina added some Haitian spice along with the lemon juice and salt and pepper on it, and let it stand for twenty minutes before adding a cup of water and placed it over the stove to simmer.

Once the food was ready, Dina set up the table and called her parents and her brother Ted to come to eat. While they were eating, her father asked her about her "other boss".

"What is all the mystery about your other boss?" asked Dina's father

"Let us just eat peacefully," requested her mother, "Dina must be exhausted, not only she did not sleep a lot last night because she had to help her employer with a sick patient, but also, she had to stand for hours to cook dinner for us."

After the dinner, Dina went to her mother to thank her for standing up for her when her father wanted to interrogate her.

"You don't have to thank me for that, I am your mother Dina; I just wish that you could be more open with me. My experiences as a woman could keep you from making a lot of mistakes."

"I know mom, I will try to remember that…" replied Dina

"Well do not wait too long baby, sometimes, a good decision can be made just by following a simple advice. I promise I won't share any of your confidential stories with your father if you do not want me to." Promise Dina's mother

"Sure, mom and thank you for always being available for me. I really mean it," added Dina. "If I don't ask you for advice, it's not because I don't trust you, it just that I don't want you to be deceived by some bad decisions that I took by following my heart instead of my brain." Avowed Dina

"Wow, are things that bad Dina?" Enquired her mother

"I really don't know any more mom. I guess it depends of how you look at them." Admitted Dina

"Well, all I know is that you have a good heart, you love your family unconditionally and you are always ready to help others. If your heart has led you towards this particular person, and you still in love with him, I'm sure this person must be somehow the right one for you." Explained her mother

"I thought he was the love of my life, until I discovered that he was the right one for some other girl also," explained Dina

"He cheated on you, right? But you know, if women were to leave their men every time they cheated, I'm sure there would be just a few women with boyfriend and husband. Anyway, most of the men that cheated often change once they exchange vows with the woman that they love. Does he want you back?" Asked her mother

"That's what he said, but I'm too scared to take a second chance with him, knowing that he could break my heart again." Avowed Dina

"If you want my advice, you should give him a second chance. Good people usually learn from their mistakes and try to make amends for the bad situations that they have caused." Explained her mother

"I just hope that you are right, mom," Replied Dina

"Well the only way to check the veracity of anything is to try it again, but this time, do it the right way, pray to God about it first; then, invite that gentleman to come to ask your father for your hand." Advised her mother

"You always knew right?" Asked Dina to her mother

"All I know is that some guy has stolen my baby girl's heart and had put her world upside down. But as you must know by now, love always comes with sacrifice. Everybody must compromise something to be able to live with the love of their life. For some people, it is their pride that they must put aside; some must renounce to their independence, and others often must abandon their comfort zone. I suspected that your pride might be the white flag that you need to surrender to give that guy a second chance. In addition, you are a Christian, forgiving should be one of your qualities, Dina." Said her mother

"I want to forgive him mom; it just that I'm not ready yet." Said Dina

"Well, take your time. If he really loves you, he will understand, and will be quietly waiting for you to forgive him. I'm certain that your love will prevail."

"Thank you, mom, I love you!" Declared Dina

"I love you too, now go to have some rest, you have been cooking for at least four hours." Said her mother

On Monday morning, when Dina went in Doctor Lawrence office to pick up some charts, he asked her if she and her brother had found any apartments in which they were interested.

"No," answered Dina, "I did not tell him about your generous proposition yet." She added

"Well don't wait any longer, if you really want to find an apartment. The sooner you start looking; the better is your chance to find a good one." Advised Gavin

"Really," replied Dina

"Yeah, trust me if you wait for the last minute when you are in a rush to search for an apartment, you might end up taking one in a neighborhood that might not be suitable for you. I have a friend of mine who is a real estate agent, I can ask him to help you." Proposed Gavin

"Well, I could definitely use some professional help on my search," said Dina

"I will give him a call to set up an appointment for you." Proposed Gavin

"Well thank you, it's really nice of you," replied Dina

"From what I see, you are a reliable employee, I think you deserve it," said Gavin

When Dina arrived at home, she went straight to her brother's room to tell him the good news. Ted was sitting aside of his bed, talking on the phone; he looked very anxious. Dina sat quietly beside him, moved the phone away from his face, and pressed the speaker button.

"…This is your baby, you are going to take your responsibility, or I will force you to; your choice!" Resonated a female's voice in the end of the line.

Dina knew instinctively that was Angel's voice.

"Oh no! Angel is pregnant…" realized Dina

"Don't worry, I will take my responsibilities." Replied Ted.

"Yeah, you better start finding a job, because you are about to be a father," insisted Angel

"I need to hang up now; I will call you later, okay?" Replied Ted

"I'm not finished, said Angel's firmly, my father said that they need a person for the laundry at the hotel were he's working; he can talk to the manager, and schedule an appointment for you if you're interested." Suggested Angel

No problem, just let me know when and where the appointment will take place, ok? I should go now, said Ted

Wait, did I tell you our conversation was over? Asked Angel

"No, I'm sorry," conceded Ted

Anyway, don't forget to call me back to enquire about the laundry job, okay? Demanded Angel

"Yeah, I will," assured Ted

"Also, don't forget to tell your parents they are going to have a grand-kid," continued Angel

"Yes, I will, but I really have to go now Angel," begged Ted

"Do not hang up on me, Ted" yelled Angel

"I will call you later Angel, I promise," assured Ted

Ted hung up the phone and hold his head in his hands.

"Angel is pregnant, isn't she?" Asked Dina

"Yeah, I'm so done," replied Ted

"Everything is going to be alright," said Dina, "it's not the end of the world you know."

"For me it is, you know how bad dad is going to react to this. He warned me so many times about Angel." Replied Ted

"Don't be bothered about how dad is going to react. Just because you are going to be a father doesn't mean that you failed. I think this baby is going to have a positive effect on you; This child will be a source of motivation for you to succeed in life. Knowing that somebody is counting on you to survive will give you the strength that you need to get out, find a job, work hard, and go back to school to not only have a better education, but also a better job to take care of that child." Said Dina

"Do you think I'm going to be a good father?" Asked Ted

"Better yet, I think you're going to be a great father," answered Dina

"What if I'm not?" Doubted Ted

"Well, nobody's perfect. If you love that child and provide for him or her, you will be just fine." Assured Dina.

"Thanks Dina. Now, I know why dad cherishes you so much, you always find a way to encourage people, specially me. I was such an idiot to envy you. I feel ashamed that I treated you the way I did." Said Ted.

"Don't be; I was not always the perfect sister also," admitted Dina

"You bet," joked Ted. "Anyway, thanks for being there when I really need you," he added

"You're welcome bro, I'm going to cook now, see you later." Replied Dina

While Dina was preparing the family meal, she was thinking about her encounter with Gavin and his proposition to co-sign an apartment lease for her brother and her to ease the process, as their income would not be enough. Now that Angel was expecting, the situation was more complicated. "Ted is going to have responsibilities, and when finally, he will find a job, his wages will probably be just enough to cover Angel and the baby's basic needs. I need to tell Gavin that my brother and I are not interested in moving out of our parents' house anymore." Thought Dina

"What I need now is to get married and move out with my husband. If only Derrick had kept the promise, he made to me two years ago; I would be happily married by now. Even though he's a cheater, I should forgive him as my mother told me, and should probably give him another chance if he's still in love with me as he pretends."

Chapter 13

Dina was still thinking about Derrick's romantic avowal when she arrived at work. His phrase resonated in her head word by word: "I'm still in love with you." If what he said is true, I will give him a second chance, but how can I verify if he's telling me the truth? He might just be pretending being in love with me as he did the first time. I don't think that he even knows what the word "love" means, giving the fact that he cannot love one girl at a time. The only thing that seems to move him is my nocturnal escapade with Dr. Lawrence. I should do that more often, so he would marry me if he ever wanted to stop us for going out together.

When Dina entered Doctor Lawrence's office, he was standing near his desk, showing a sonography picture of a patient to Doctor Lee.

"Good morning!" Said Dina, with a seductive smile.

"Good morning!" answered both.

"I came to see if you didn't need anything, Doctor Lawrence," said Dina

"Well I'm all set for now," answered Gavin.

"Perfect, do not hesitate to call me if you need anything," proposed Dina, while touching his arm lightly.

"Okay... I will certainly try to remember that," Replied Gavin.

"Good, I'm going to see if Edna needs any help at the front office then"

Dina left the room and closed the door.

Gavin was thinking, "Dina is still in love with Derrick, she's flirting with me to make him jealous."

"Try to remember what Gavin! Focus, don't you see what she's doing, she's just using you to make me jealous." Insinuated Derrick

"It is so obvious that even Derrick can see it," thought Gavin. "But why is derrick so panicked by the fact that Dina is using me to make him jealous? Can it be that he suspected that Dina is in fact in love with me, but wants to get revenge against him so bad that she doesn't even realize that?" So, he decided to confront Derrick

"Maybe, maybe not; it's fifty- fifty Derrick, and I refuse to let you captivate my mind by implying she's seducing me to get you back." Replied Gavin

"You know what, you're right; it's fifty-fifty. But don't forget, you're playing with fire. Do not blame me when you get your heart broken because sooner or later, you will realize that I'm the one that she loves when she dumps you." Said Derrick

"Why would I blame it on you Derrick, I'm an adult and I'm allowed to use fire without any supervision. I'm perfectly aware of the risk that I'm taking." Replied Gavin

"I'm sure you do, I hope you will remember that when you are invited to our wedding. Don't get attached to her, because I'm the one that she wants to be with." Declared Derrick

"Here we go again! Listen, I think it's ridiculous for you and me to keep fighting over Dina. She's the one that's making her choice let's make a truce and see what is going to happen, okay?" Proposed Gavin

"Fine with me, I already know who she's going to choose, and it's not you." Argued Derrick

Without replying to Derrick, Gavin picked up his phone, and dialed the front office extension. When Edna answered, he asked Edna how many pharmaceutical sales representatives that were expected to come for the day.

"Only three pharmaceutical representatives are expected today," Replied Edna

"Good, just make sure they have brought some brochures and medications samples before allowing them in my office. I would like to have several patients' feedbacks before prescribing some of the new medications. What is Mrs. Joseph doing?" Asked Gavin

"She was on the computer checking the kind of visits that each patient has for their appointment today; now, she went to the exam rooms to place some syringes and bandages. Do you want me to send her to you?" Asked Edna

"Not right now, but tell her to call the pharmacy to refill Mrs. Altagracia Maduro's prescription," instructed Dr. Lawrence

"Ok, replied Edna," anything else?

"One last thing", added Doctor Lawrence, "Mrs. Yvrose Lherisson has requested a copy of her medical records, can you ask Mrs. Joseph to print it for her?"

"Sure," answered Edna.

"That will be all for now," said Doctor Lawrence before hanging up the phone.

"It seems like you are going to keep her busy today, what is the purpose of all this?" Asked Derrick?

"I am just trying to work peacefully without having to argue with you over Dina, Derrick. I'm sure that knowing that she won't be in my office any time soon today will make you very happy. Now if you'll excuse me, I need to make some calls." Said Gavin

After Dina finished to place the syringes and the bandages in the exam rooms, she realized that there were only a few gowns in room two, she went back to pick up some more at the storage room. While she was in the storage room, Edna opened the door and told her that Dr. Lawrence wanted her to call the pharmacy to refill Mrs. Altagracia Maduro's prescriptions, and to print a copy of Mrs. Yvrose Lherisson medical records for her.

"Wow, calling pharmacy, and printing medical record? it's like Dr. Lawrence wants me to stay away from him; well he won't have to beg me for that, if Derrick is still into me, I'm all good," thought Dina.

After further thinking, Dina realized that Dr. Lawrence avoiding her might be the work of Derrick. He must have said something to Dr. Lawrence that caused him to react like that. I must find a way to make him need my service as much as before, is Derrick trying to get me fired? I would not be surprise if it's the case. Definitely, Derrick is always the source of my problems.

"I'm Happy that Gavin is devoted to leave Dina alone... at least for the entire day," thought Derrick. "I want to show him how much I appreciate it. Let me ask him to join me in my house like the old times, just him and I. If he accepted, not only we would spend some time together and erase those clouds that are hanging between us, but also, I would be certain that he's not with Dina."

Therefore, when it was time to go home, Derrick invited Gavin to the chalet that he has just brought. No, thank you; maybe another day said Gavin, I'm going home, take a hot shower, and go to bed.

"Too bad answered Dina I was going to ask you if you needed company.

"Oh, would you be interested to accompany me? Asked Gavin

"Certainly" answered Dina, "if I'm not imposing." She added

"You're not," said Gavin, "it would be my pleasure. As long as I am not being use as a bait."

"A bait, you? Why would you think that, that's very rude; I just wanted to be useful, you barely ask me to do any task for you today," explained Dina

"I'm sorry if I hurt your feelings, but I had to make sure that it was not the case. Anyway, speaking about accompanying me, I'm going to the gynecologists' convention, it's an annual meeting which will be held in France this year for three days; it's in two weeks, and I'm in need of an assistant. I'm sorry to give you such a short notice but I hope that you will be able to make this business trip with me." Proposed Gavin

"Sure, it will be an honor for me Doctor Lawrence." Then, Dina turned to Derrick, and asked

"Are you participating at the convention too Doctor Lee?"

"Unfortunately, no, not this one; but there will be many other opportunities for you to travel with me before long." Answered Derrick

"Let me remind you that Ms. Joseph is *my* medical assistant, Edna should be the one to accompany you, Derrick, not Dina," said Gavin, annoyed.

"Oh yeah, I thought Dina was hired by the medical office that *we* shared together," argued Derrick

"Come on Derrick, you're the one that suggested me to hire *my own* medical assistant because Edna is *your* private medical assistant, and should prioritize the tasks that *you* give her? Your words Derrick, not mine! You know what, just look at the copy of Edna's contract when you have time." Replied Gavin

"What about we look at Dina's contract instead, it's about her after all; does Dina's contract stipule that she's your private medical assistant?" Asked Derrick

"That's a good question, what's your take on it, Dina?" Asked Gavin

"I don't know, I didn't go over my contract at all, I just signed it and returned it to you. I was so happy to find this job, that it was not one of my concerns, as you might remember Doctor Lawrence," avowed Dina, confused.

In one hand, Dina wanted to go to the convention with Gavin, and in the other hand, she wanted to stay close to Derrick and work on their issues until maybe he marries her.

"Really Dina! Exclaimed Derrick, you were once a law student, you are aware that you are supposed to read every document before you sign it; how can you be so careless? However, I'm not sure that you have any obligation to travel with Gavin. If you want, I can get my lawyers to look over your contract for you." Proposed Derrick

"No, there's no need for that Doctor Lee. I'm very excited to be Doctor Lawrence's assistant at this convention. It's going to be my first, and as I said before, I feel honored to be chosen." Replied Dina

"You're welcome, but I did not choose you, fate brought you to me, Dina; it just happens that I'm happy about the outcome, you are really a hard-working person." Said Gavin.

"Thank you, Doctor Lawrence," expressed Dina. "Goodbye," she added to the attention of both, before leaving the office to go home.

Two weeks later, Dina was on a plane to Lyon, France. They boarded their first plane from Baltimore Washington International airport, at 7 p.m.

After a short stop at the Keflavik International Airport, they boarded the second plane and arrived at Lyon Saint-Exupery Airport LYS Lyon, France at 11:30 in the morning. The hotel's pickup driver was waiting outside the airport for them and drove them to the hotel.

Because Gavin had a reservation, the check-in process was straight forward. Upon arrivals, the front desk agent, a tall white older man who seemed to be in his 60s and spoke English very well, greeted them with a pleasant smile and presented the registration card to Gavin and Dina to sign. Gavin handed his credit card to the front desk agent, he swiped the card, and gave it back to Gavin. After handing the card keys of their respective rooms to them, the front desk agent called the bellboy to carry their luggage's to their rooms.

"I will let you settle down, and I will see you in one hour at the meeting room." Said Gavin

Dina's room was colorful. It was equipped with all the necessary supplies, from a complementary mini bar with free soft drinks, to a large bathroom with shower and bathtub. In the bathroom, was hanging a bath towel and two washcloths. Two more towels were elegantly placed on the towel rack. Dina looked at the sink area, and saw bar soap, shampoo, conditioner. On another corner of the sink were placed many other luxury toiletries such as mouthwash, lotion, cotton ball, and face tissue.

Dina sat on the bed and felt how comfy it was. The room's furniture was very nice. Dina went to open the curtains and looked at the window, she discovered that her room had a very nice view of the street. Then, she went to open the closet, and saw a bathrobe hanging inside, along with an iron and an iron board. "Wow," thought Dina, "this hotel is very luxurious, Doctor Lawrence must have paid a tidy sum of money for these rooms."

Gavin's room was close to the meeting room. As he had asked Dina to meet him there, she washed her face, grabbed a soda from the mini bar in her room, drink some, and left to go to the meeting room. The meeting room was very spacious, with a podium in the middle and upholstered chairs arranged in rows. Gavin was sitting in one of the chairs in the back of the room and waved at Dina. She went to him and sat on a chair beside him.

"I just wanted to give you your travel allowance, so you can shop around tomorrow, the conference is in two days." Said Gavin, while handing a white envelope to Dina

"Thank you very much," said Dina.

"You're welcome." Answered Gavin, "are you comfortable in your room," he asked

"Yes, it's very convenient, I have all the necessary items there." Explained Dina

"Well I'm happy that you like it. See you tomorrow morning then." Said Gavin

Dina left and went back to her room. Once inside, she opened the envelope, and found one thousand and five hundred dollars. After counting the money, she washed her hands and went to binge watch the TV. After a while, Dina who did not sleep at all on the plane was very tired, she went to brush her teeth, took a shower, prayed to God, and went to sleep.

Dina woke up the next morning and went for a walk. She discovered that the hotel was from a walking distance of many stores and restaurants. She went to the stores, and brought a perfume for her mother, a watch for her father, and a shirt for her brother with the money from the travel allowance payment that Gavin gave her.

The next morning, she rejoined Gavin at the meeting room to discuss about the last-minute details of the conference's schedule. Gavin handed Dina a pen and a notebook and told her that she needed them to take notes for him at the conference, and that he would be expecting a written report at the end of the conference. Before ending their meeting, Gavin asked:

"How is your apartment search going? My friend told me that he tried to contact you, but you were not available."

"Yes, I found his message, I did not reply to him yet because unfortunately, I must postpone the apartment search." Said Dina

"Really? for how long?" Asked Gavin

"I'm not sure… maybe next year," replied Dina

"Next year? you seemed to be really motivated to get your own place, what happened?" Said Gavin

"Something inopportune had happened, that force me to change my plan." Avowed Dina

"Well, if it has something to do with your income, I can help you financially until you get on your feet." Proposed Gavin

"It's more complicated than that, but thank you Doctor Lawrence." Said Dina

"Do you want to talk about it?" Insisted Gavin

"No, not now…" replied Dina

"Okay, but I want you to know that I'm available anytime that you're ready to discuss about it," said Gavin

"Okay thank you," answered Dina.

After that, they left the meeting room area, and went back to their respective rooms.

Gavin and Dina were very busy with the convention for the rest of the days. The first day, Dina had to take notes at the coding seminar about updates on the CPT coding skills for the practice. The second day, she and Gavin attended a seminar on pregnancy complications. The last day, they attended the practice essentials seminar.

When Dina arrived at home from her trip, she found her parents and her brother Ted sitting on the family room. Ted was holding a white paper in his hand.

"I'm happy to see you too!" said Dina ironically, as they did not greet her as usual. "Is this mail for me?" She asked while pointing at the white paper in Ted's hands

"No," replied Ted, "it's a letter that Angel has sent to me, informing me that she will be starting a child support process against me as soon as she gives birth."

"That's impossible, I thought that you gave her your word that you will take your responsibilities?" Said Dina

"Apparently, she does not trust me, she is just pressuring me." Replied Ted

"What is wrong with Angel? Have you ever lied to her about anything before?" Asked Dina

"No, not as far as I can remember; but she said that's the only way to be certain that I would get out and find a job before the baby arrives, can you believe that? Replied Ted

"Actually, I can believe that, we are speaking about Angel after all. Don't you remember the way that she had thrown us out of her house? I'm telling you, that girl is senseless." Said Dina

After the convention trip, Gavin allowed Dina to stay at home for two days to get some rest and recover from the time difference. Dina profited to put the notes that she took at the conference together and type the written report for Gavin.

When she went back to work, the atmosphere was very tense at the office. Gavin and Derrick hardly spoke to each other. At lunch time, Dina went to the refrigerator and took the boiled yam and the herring sauce that she brought from home. She was going to put it in the microwave, when she saw Derrick coming. She sidled past him, pretending that she had not seen him.

"Look who finally came to work!" Said ironically Derrick

"Doctor Lawrence allowed me to stay at home for two days," explained Dina

"I get that part, but I don't know why you guys stayed at the hotel for six days, when the convention was only for three days." Said Derrick

"Oh, we arrived two days early and stayed one day late," explained Dina

"Exactly!" Exclaimed Derrick

"It's not what you think," said Dina, once she realized what Derrick was insinuating.

"Well it certainly looks like," argued Derrick. "Do you care to tell me what you guys did during these three other days?"

"Personally, I slept the first day, then I went to shop. The second day, Doctor Lawrence and I had a last-minute meeting in preparation of the convention." Explained Dina.

"What about the last day?" Asked Derrick

"Doctor Lawrence was socializing with his old friends and other physicians, while I was preparing my luggage to come back home; mystery solve!" joked Dina

"I'm serious Dina, this cannot continue. Gavin hired you as a medical assistant for this practice, I don't know why you are always somewhere with him, when you two are not on a date at a nightclub, you are on a so-called business trip. Why can't he just let you be a normal medical assistant?" Said Derrick

"So, I am not a *normal* medical assistant?" Asked Dina

"Oh, do not twist my words around, Dina, you know perfectly what I mean!" exclaimed Derrick

"No, I cannot read your mind, Derrick, how could I possibly know what you mean? If I were able to read your mind, I would have known that you were cheating on me the very first day that you started" replied Dina

"I know what you are doing, Dina, you are trying to change the subject of this conversation because something happened between Gavin and you, and you feel embarrassed to talk about it." Said Derrick

"No, not at all, nothing happened between Doctor Lawrence and I. Doctor Lawrence is a perfect gentleman, he would not prey on his employee at the first occasion that he had. Now that I gave you all the details about the trip, can I please reheat my food? I'm hungry." Said Dina.

"Go ahead," said Derrick "I hope that you are telling the truth, because if something happened between you two, I will make you regret it, Dina: I will make you regret it so bad!" he added. Then, he turned around and left.

After the argument she had with Derrick, Dina's appetite was gone. She placed her food back into the refrigerator and decided to go for a short walk.

When she came back, she felt more energized and less irritated.

Chapter 14

The following week, it was very busy at the office. Dina and Edna had to help Gavin and Derrick disinfect many reusable medical equipment including the speculums that they used to perform pelvic exams. Dina learned how to properly follow reprocessing procedures to lower the possibilities of cross-contamination.

Dina was in Gavin's office, sorting some of his patients' charts, when Edna came to say goodbye, Dina looked at her watch and saw that it was already 6 p.m. She picked up her handbag and left. Once outside, near her car, she opened her bag to take out her keys. While searching inside it, she felt that someone was behind her, she turned back immediately; it was Derrick.

"Hi," said Derrick "I was looking for you, Edna told me that you had finished early today, where were you?"

"I was in Doctor Lawrence's office; he needed me to sort some patients' charts for him." Answered Dina.

"I see, I have a surprise for you" he said, "I just want you to take your car, and follow mine until we get there."

"I'm really tired tonight, you'll have to wait for tomorrow; all I want to do right now is to take a shower and go straight to bed." responded Dina, while continuing to search her bag for her keys.

"Sounds great to me," replied Derrick, "Come on follow me" he added.

"I want to go home, in my own bed, all alone, Derrick," Said Dina who finally found her keys.

Derrick snatched the keys from her, walked towards his car, and instructed her to follow him.

"Please Derrick, give me my keys." Said desperately Dina.

Derrick headed to his car, opened the driver's door, and directed her to enter. Dina tried to resist claiming that her parents were waiting for her, but Derrick closed the door and said:

"Here's my key, just follow me; it won't be long, I promise."

He then went back to Dina's car, opened the door, sat behind the wheel and drove away.

Dina did not have any choice than to follow him. He arrived in front of a restaurant, slowed down and honked at Dina, signaling her to park.

After locating an empty place to park her car, Dina got out to look for Derrick. She found him standing near the restaurant entry, waiting for her.

"What took you so long," he asked.

"I was looking for a vacant parking space, obviously finding one here is not easy." Retorted Dina

He entered with her inside the restaurant; a brunet woman who wore a name tag with the name of "Jessie" accompanied them to their table.

"Derrick had everything planned," thought Dina. "I think he is about to propose to me."

Derrick took Dina's hand, and walked her to their table. A server came to take their order. Dina chose a Caesar salad, and Derrick order scallops with rice. The server left and came back with a plate of tossed garlic bread. Dina opened the bread container to take a piece of bread, and a ring was shining in top. Derrick took the ring, presented it to Dina, and asked her to marry him.

"Well, said Dina, if you really serious about marrying me, I want us to do it the right way this time. You would have to go to ask my hands to my parents', and then formally present me to yours." Replied Dina

"Of course," acquiesced Derrick, "we should do that, is that a yes?" he asked

"It is." Replied Dina

Derrick put the ring on Dina's finger, and they continued to eat peacefully. Dina was surprised to feel so empty even though Derrick just proposed to her. She thought that when this day had finally arrived, she would be thrilled.

The same week, Derrick presented Dina to his parent's, and told them that he was in love with her and wanted to marry her. Even though Derrick's parents were complaining that Derrick's visit was more about letting them know that he was getting married than asking for their approval to marry Dina, they give them their support and told him that they were happy that he had decided to settle down.

Dina was happy that finally she was getting married and leaving her parent's house. Yet, she felt bad that Gavin will not be a part of her life anymore, and she did not know how to tell him the news.

"I better be the first one to tell him about it, because Derrick might try to throw our wedding news in Gavin's face as a victory." Thought Dina.

Dina went to work before time the next day, she knew that Gavin liked to be at the office early in the morning to make sure that everything is well set, and to catch the early calls of patients who want to get an appointment on the same day.

When Dina arrived, the office was quiet. If she did not see Gavin's car in the parking lot, she would have thought that he was not there. Dina placed her handbag inside a drawer at the reception and went to place her lunch into the refrigerator. As she was closing the refrigerator door, she heard Gavin calling her from his office.

Dina went to his office and knocked at the half-opened door.

"Come on in," answered Gavin, "is everything okay at your house, you are so early this morning," he enquired

"Yes," answered Dina, "I just wanted to come early today to take care of some private business," she added

"Oh, really?" asked Gavin "It must be something very important to you…, well…, I guess I will let you… go…do your things, then," stammered Gavin

Gavin was concerned, what kind of personal business could Dina possibly have to take care of at the office, besides seeing Derrick. Gavin wanted to ask Dina if she came early to meet Derrick, but the words just would not pass his lips.

Dina did not move, she did not know how to explain to Gavin that she came to work early just to talk to him. "He seems very nervous," thought Dina, "I'm not sure if it is the right time to have a conversation with him about Derrick and me."

Gavin's emotion was distracting him from what was happening around him, he was staring into space and did not notice that Dina was still standing in front of him. Once he realized that, he said to her:

"I'm sorry, I thought I said that you could go back to whatever you were doing."

"Yes, you did, it's just that…" said Dina

"Derrick is not here yet… you came here early so you could chat with him, right?" Asked Gavin

"No, it's not the case at all, I know that Doctor Lee never comes early to the office…" replied Dina

"So, you came early to plan a surprise for him," deduced Gavin

"No…! Can I ask you a question Doctor Lawrence?" asked Dina

"Sure, what is it?" replied Gavin, who nod his head slightly.

"Why did you invite me to dance the first time at the nightclub?"

"Beside the fact that you looked desperate?" He joked

"I didn't look desperate," argued Dina

"Okay, if you said so, but I know what I saw. You looked vulnerable and nostalgic, all at the same time." Said Gavin

"Well, all of this still doesn't explain why you came to me. Were you on a mission to save girls that appeared vulnerable and nostalgic?" Asked Dina

"I don't think so; I was instead attracted to a beautiful girl sitting alone that was looking at other couples dancing. I observed you, and you were looking with admiration at your two friends dancing on the dance floor. I said to myself this is the kind of person that I'm looking for, a girl who like to see people falling in love might be looking for love also, and nothing else." Replied Gavin.

"Wow, did you say you were attracted? I don't seem to be the kind of woman that would attract you." Said Dina

"What do you think you know about the kind of woman I'm attracted to?"

"Well, when I was at the university, guys like you mostly went out with people from their own race," said Dina

Maybe that was the kind of woman that they liked. Derrick was at the same university as you, and he went out with you. As for me, *you are* the kind of woman that I like." Replied Gavin

"No, I'm not your type. I'm just a toy that you want, but you cannot have… yet. If you ever got me, you would play with me and throw me away just as Derrick did" Said Dina.

"Have you ever learned that people are unique, therefore you are not supposed to compare them?" Replied Gavin. "So, please stop comparing me to Derrick. Also, if I wanted you as a toy like you said, I would probably find myself an imitation of you. We are not out of stock of black women in this country, aren't we? You are special in my eyes, and you will always be, believe it or not. The only person who is playing with you as if you were a toy is your beloved ex-boyfriend, but you are too blinded by your love for him to realize that. Let me give you an advice: If you want him to take you seriously, stop throwing yourself at him, as you do every time he's around." He added

"Me, I don't throw myself at him. Do I…?" asked Dina

"Oh yeah, you should see yourself when you are doing it, the way that you turned around him as if you were waiting for him to touch you. Also, the way that you look at him, it's like you just want him to kiss you. Unfortunately, he's not the only one around who can detect that.

"Unfortunately?" Repeated Dina.

"Yeah, unfortunately," confirmed Gavin.

"Why? Does it interfere with my performance as your employee?" Asked Dina

"Believe me, I wish it was that simple." Replied Gavin.

"So, if it does not affect my work efficiency, why does it matter to you?" said Dina.

"You really want to know?" asked Gavin.

"Well you seem very concerned about it. As your employee, I need to know what it is, so I can modify properly the way that I act around him at your office." Explained Dina

"Only at the office?" asked Gavin.

"Well, this is mostly the place where I see him. Anyway, I'm willing to change my behavior near him anywhere, if you tell me why it matters so much to you." Said Dina.

"Is that a promise?" Asked Gavin

"Maybe," replied Dina, "just tell me, and I will see what I can do about it," she added

"Well, it matters to me because I have to witness the woman that I love teasing another man that doesn't care about her as much as I do." Said Gavin

"The woman that you love?" Repeated Dina; why is it so easy for men to lie about loving a woman, when in fact, love is the last thing that crosses their minds."

"So, you don't believe that I really love you?" asked Gavin

"No, but it doesn't matter anyway," replied Dina

"It matters to me, maybe I should prove it to you," said Gavin

"How," replied Dina, "by telling me how hard it is for you to witness me flirting with Derrick?"

"No, I was thinking about kissing you." Said Gavin

"What? I don't think it's a good idea," replied Dina

"Why not?" Asked Gavin, while getting closer to her

"Because it's too personal, worse you might not like it." Argued Dina

"It's not like I never kissed you before." Said Gavin

"But you never…" started Dina, then again, Gavin interrupted her

"Yes, I did, you just don't remember. Let me refresh your memory, it was our first date, in your house; you were crying and had mascara all over your face." Replied Gavin

"Yeah, I remember, but it was an innocent kiss of comfort on my forehead." Said Dina

"So, you do remember? It still counts as a kiss for me." Replied Gavin

Dina smiled. How could she ever forget about this warm kiss that he put on her forehead? Definitely, Gavin knew how to act as a true sensitive person. "If it's a game that he's playing with me, he is largely winning," thought Dina. He knew exactly what to say, but more importantly when to say it; and his words were like a caress to her whole body. "If only my life wasn't so complicated with my past with Derrick. "Derrick…" thought Dina, "I almost forget to tell Gavin that I'm getting married to Derrick."

"I have something to tell you; in fact, I wanted to be the first person to tell you that; Derrick and I are getting married. He proposed last night, and I said yes." Said Dina

Gavin was so close to kiss her that he had to take a few steps backward to get away from her.

"Wow… congratulations," said Gavin, surprised; "I hope that you find happiness in your sweet revenge plot." He added

"I was expecting you to react like that Doctor Lawrence," replied Dina

"Well you sure are my opposite Dina, you are so unpredictable; how can you marry him when you know that you don't love him?" Said Gavin

"I'm not the first person on earth that would marry someone for the wrong reason, and surely, I'm not going to be the last one either. Yes, I accepted to marry him to compensate the shame that he brought on me two years ago, but what about him, don't you know why he's marrying me?" Asked Dina

"No, but I'm sure you are going to tell me," replied Gavin

"He's marrying me because he thinks that you want me, and because all of his friends are getting married now, I'm the only woman that he knows he can cheat on and come back as he wishes, aren't those reasons to marry someone also wrong? But you seem more preoccupied by my intentions than his," accused Dina

"I'm more interested in yours because you are the one that struggled for two years to get over him, which you never did as he claimed."

"You know I'm over him! I'm marrying him to get revenge as you like to point out." Maintained Dina

"Well good luck with that." Replied Gavin.

Dina went back to her duties. Gavin could not wait for Derrick to come to work to talk to him. Right away, he called Derrick and tried to convince him to leave Dina alone.

"You know you're incapable of staying with one woman at a time, why marrying Dina?" Asked Gavin

"Come on, you're a guy and I'm sure you realized how much I want her. Since she went back to her Christian girl life, she refuses to let me touch her, calling that a sin, and telling me that she won't do anything without getting married. Now, she calls it a sin. There is no other solution than marrying her." Explained Derrick.

Gavin was tossing and turning in his bed, he could not sleep at all that night. He realized how much he was in love with Dina and could not resolve to see her marrying someone who just wanted her body as Derrick was, unlike him who love her madly.

Chapter 15

When finally, the night was over, and the sun came up, Gavin decided to go to see Dina to try to dissuade her from marrying Derrick. When Gavin arrived at Dina's house, the family car was not parked in the garage. "Maybe she's not here," thought Gavin." Let me knock anyway." Gavin was about to knock at the entrance door when he refrained himself from doing so. "What am I doing here? it's way too early to come to someone's house." He backtracked in haste to go to his car.

Gavin was a few meters away from his car when he heard someone shouting his name. when he turned around, he discovered that was Dina's mother. She was wearing a dressing gown and her hair was wrapped in a sleep cap. Dina's mother was holding a black metal watering can in her right hand and was waiving at Gavin with her left one.

"Doctor Lawrence, what a wonderful surprise! I was about to water the flowers when I saw you, come on in," said Dina's mother. "Dina is in her room, she's still sleeping; do you want me to wake her up?" She asked with her Haitian accent.

"No Mrs. Joseph, it's not that urgent, I can… come back later." Said Gavin nervously

"Correct me if I'm wrong but I'm sure you would have not come if it was not very important. So, Doctor Lawrence, would you be kind enough to tell me what is going on?" Asked Dina's mother. "Please," she added.

"It is about your daughter's wedding, I need to talk to her," avowed Gavin.

Immediately, Mrs. Joseph's eyes opened wider, her mouth dropped open. She was totally surprised and could not believe her ears; her daughter was about to get married and she had to learn about it from someone else.

Seeing that Mrs. Joseph looked surprised, Gavin decided to check if whether she knew about it.

"Didn't your daughter tell you that she is about to get married?" Asked Gavin

"No, she only said that she has something to announce today when all of us will be there. So, you are here to ask for her hands? Is she pregnant?" Asked her mother

"No, not to my knowledge, Mrs., Joseph," replied Gavin

"Well, why are you two in such a hurry to tie the knots? I understand that you two have a history, but I think that you should take it slowly this time." Said her mother

"I'm sorry to have not come up to your expectations Mrs. Joseph, but unfortunately it is not me, your daughter is marrying someone else." Replied Gavin

"I see, I'm sorry for assuming it was you, but who is this man? I am pretty sure that you know who he is." Said Dina's mother

"I think you should ask Dina, she is the one that should tell you about this gentleman." Replied Gavin

"I know it might sound stupid, but I would rather want to see her being with you." Said her mother

"Your daughter is an incredible young woman, I am sure she will bring you a suitable son- in- law." Replied Gavin

"You are in love with her, aren't you?" Asked Dina's mother

"Indeed, Mrs. Joseph, but still, I am not the lucky one. The truth is, I came here to attempt to discourage your daughter from marrying someone else." Said Gavin

"In this case, I think I better wake her up right now." Replied Mrs. Joseph

"Dina's mother went to her daughter's room and opened the curtains; automatically, the sunlight streamed into Dina's room. Then, her mother went to her bed, and pulled the cover away from her.

"Mom, what are you doing?" complained Dina

"As you can see, I am waking you up," said her mother

"But why, I don't have to go to work, today it's Sunday mom," continued Dina

"I know, but you have a visitor, he has been waiting for you for some time now." Replied her mother.

"Me? I am not expecting anybody, who would come to someone's house this early?" Moaned Dina

"Why don't you come with me to see?" proposed her mother

"Come on mom! Why are you making all this mystery for a visitor?" asked Dina

"The same way that you have kept a secrecy about your groom to be," replied her mother.

Dina was surprised, she did not yet have the chance to tell her family that she was getting married. Now that her mother learned it from somebody, she felt ashamed.

"I was going to tell everybody when I got the chance. I just didn't find any favorable occasion yet." Said Dina

"Well, I think it is an appropriate time today to tell us. By the way, there is a fine young man sitting at this moment in our living room, and he is desperately in love with you. I hope that you will seize your chance with him." Replied her mother

She went with Dina, left her in the living room with Gavin and asked: "Would you like some coffee, Doctor Lawrence?"

"No, Mrs. Joseph, but thank you. I will be leaving in a few minutes, I have caused you enough trouble for today." Replied Gavin

"Not at all," replied Dina's mother; "it was a pleasure talking to you. I will be in the kitchen if you need anything." She added before leaving.

As soon as Dina's mother's left, Dina turned towards Gavin and asked:

"Doctor Lawrence, what are you doing here? And why would you tell my mother about my wedding?"

"I apologize. I wanted to talk to you about your decision to marry Derrick." Replied Gavin

"We had already talked about it. I have not changed my mind concerning this matter and will probably not change it." Said Dina

"You know perfectly that wedding would be a big mistake with undesirable consequences. How could you go back to Derrick, after all he did to you?" Asked Gavin. "I was willing to marry you, I love you Dina." He added

"You were willing to marry me? Why would I marry you? Are you the first man that I made love with? no! Derrick is! He is the one that took my innocence; he should be the one to marry me." Replied Dina, hysterically.

"Do you still love him?" Asked Gavin

"I was in love with him when he broke my heart; now, I have enough hate for him to protect my feelings. He is the one that woke up the woman in me, why should I become another man's wife?" Replied Dina

"Because you should marry someone that you're in love with, Dina, not for revenge," advised Gavin

"It is easy for you to say, you are a man." Argued Dina

"We all have feelings Dina, regarding our gender or our ethnicity; so, I'm not different from you in this matter. Do you imagine what it would be for you to live with a man that you don't love, while sharing the same roof and the same bed as him? You better think about all the consequences that all of these will have on your life." Added Gavin.

"I will manage." Replied Dina

"Well, at least I have tried. Have a nice day and say bye to your mother for me."

Dina's mother was sitting in the kitchen, drinking some coffee when she heard the entrance door opened and closed. "Doctor Lawrence had left," she thought. "I think it's time to have a serious conversation with Dina." She went to the living room and saw Dina looking at Gavin Lawrence by the window. He was opening his car to drive away.

Dina startled when she heard her mother's footsteps. She turned around and seeing the look on her mother's face, she tried to escape to her room.

"Not so fast young lady, we need to talk," said her mother.

"Sure, mom; what do you want to know?"

"Why don't you sit here, next to me?" Asked her mother

"Yes, mom," replied Dina, who went to sit beside her mother.

"So, what do you want to know, mom?" Asked Dina

"Everything that you have been hiding from us. Why don't you start by revealing me the identity of this estrange man that you are about to marry?" Said her mother

"His name is Derrick Lee…" started Dina

"Well, continue," urged her mother, "where did you two met?" she asked

"He was a graduating student in medical when I was a freshman in law, at the Colossal University." Replied Dina

"A graduating student in medical, three years ago? He must be Doctor Lawrence's associate, right?" asked her mother

"Yes, that's him," confirmed Dina

"Why didn't you just leave the job when you discovered that he was one of your bosses?" Asked her mother

"He persuaded me to stay, and, I felt like it was not fair that I have to renounce at a job that I really love because of him, right after I dropped out of the University because of him." Replied Dina

"I agree with you on that one, but Dina, why do you want to marry that guy after all the trouble he had caused you?" Said her mother

"Maybe to save my honor, or to be able to leave home and get my own place, I don't know mom, I have made so many mistakes with him that I just want to erase some of them." Replied Dina

"Dina, I have taught you the word of God, you know that, if we bring our mistakes and sins to the Lord in Jesus-Christ, he can erase them for us. Trying to expunge our iniquities by ourselves would just make them messier. Have you ever tried to use an eraser to correct an error that you have made while writing on a paper, but then realized that the eraser had made the paper become more hideous than before? It is the same thing when we are trying to fix everything by ourselves, without consulting the Lord to know how to do it properly, we just keep on getting ourselves deeper and deeper in our messes." Said her mother

"You're right mom. From now on, I will make sure that I pray to God before taking any decision." Replied Dina

"Now tell me a little bit about him. How does he look? I hope he's cute, because you chose him over Doctor Lawrence, who, by the way, is a handsome and nice young man." Said her mother

"Well he looks good to me; although I never compared him to Doctor Lawrence, I think he's also cute." Replied Dina

"That's good, it's more encouraging, and when are you going to bring him home, then?" Asked her mother

"He is coming here this afternoon, mom, that's what I wanted to announce to everybody." Said Dina

In the afternoon, Derrick came as planned, and met with Dina's family.

After he left, Dina said to her parents:

"Now that I introduced Derrick to you, it's time for us to start preparing the wedding."

"Hold your horses Dina! Don't you care about what we think?" Said her father

"Of course, I do, dad; go ahead, tell me what you think, so we can move forward." Replied Dina

"I don't really like that guy, he sounds very arrogant and full of himself. Doctor Lawrence sat here and talked about himself, and never gave me the impression that he was bragging; but that guy really gets on my nerves. In my opinion, he was just showing off, and it's a clear sign that he is a self- centered person. I would not advise you to marry someone like that, because when it is time to take any important family decision, you won't matter; it will be all about him." Warned her father. Then, he turned to Dina's mother, and asked:

"What about you honey, what do you think about him?"

"I can deal with the arrogance part, it is not the first time that I have been around a conceit person. My only concern is the fact that he is not like us Dina, he's white."

"What do you mean mom, why is his color a problem for you?" Asked Dina

"No, it's not a problem for me, however, it is a problem for you, Dina." Replied her mother

"I still don't get it mom," Said Dina, confused

"Well. Let me break it down for you; many men think that they are superior to women, and as you must know, some white people really think they are superior to other races, including blacks; as a black woman, you must know that if you chose a white man as your husband, you are in double jeopardy. Not only you will have to fight to show him that you are his equal partner as a woman, but also, you will have to make a great effort to prove to him that there is nothing superior in his color." Explained her mother

"I understand very well what you are saying, and I can assure you that Derrick is not a racist." Replied Dina

"How well do you think you know this man, to be certain that he is not a racist, Dina? he cheated on you, treated you like you were his mistress, and he is the most arrogant person that I ever met. There is a good chance that he is also a bigot." Said her mother.

"What you are saying is wrong mom. As your children, we believe everything that you tell us, and when you brainwash us with your prejudice against other races, whether they are black, white, yellow or red; we started being hostile to these people, and the circle continues. Should I remind you that Doctor Lawrence is also white, you did not seem to have a problem with that." Replied Dina

"Doctor Lawrence is a decent young man who is humble and well-educated. I did not hear him brag at all. But it doesn't seem like you're interested in him, so, let's talk about your husband-to-be, have you even been presented to his family? Anyway, if they are so self-promoting as he is, I don't think they will welcome you to their clan." Said her mother

"Why does it matter, mom, whether they accept me or not? Daddy's family is black like us, and they did not accept you! But that did not keep you from marrying dad." Replied Dina

"Wow Dina, that was so rude, you had to bring that in our conversation." Said her mother

"I'm sorry mom, I was just trying to explain to you that it doesn't matter whether his family likes me or not. People will always find all kinds of crazy reasons to pretend that they are superior to others. Whether it is money, education, race, or gender there is always something that gives people with prejudice a pretext to think that they are worthwhile than they really are. I'm like you mom, people with preconception will not keep me from marrying my beau." Maintained Dina

"Sounds like you don't need our permission to marry that guy, Dina." Argued her father.

"Your father is absolutely right," replied her mother. "However, what I find more outrageous is the fact that I never heard you saying that you love that guy during this whole conversation. You are talking about the man that you plan to marry, and you cannot say once that you love him? That gives me a lot to think about, Dina." Said her mother

"I'm not sure what saying that I love him would prove, mom. I have never heard you saying how much you love dad, but I know that you love him." Replied Dina

"Exactly, Dina, you and Ted are my witnesses, you can vouch for me that I love your father by the way I treat him. But Dina you don't have any witness to vouch for you, so just tell us that you love this man, I will take your word." Said her mother

"I… I don't know what to say mom…" replied Dina

"It's simple Dina, just say that you love the man that you are about to marry," said her mother

"It's not exactly what I feel right now, but I used to feel that way about him. It still means something, right?" replied Dina

"Listen to yourself, Dina, since when have you become this cold and calculated person? It's true that I don't like that guy because of his arrogance, but it would not be fair to him to let you two get married when you know perfectly that you are not in love with him." Said her father

"He doesn't care that I'm not in love with him, dad, he just wants us to get married," replied Dina

"In that case, I don't have any other choice than to not give you my permission to marry him. I don't know what kind of game that you two are playing but I don't want to be a part of it. Marriage is a serious act and should be respected as such.

"Mom," Said Dina, "can you please talk to dad?"

"I'm sorry Dina, but I have to side with your father on that one. I have always dreamt of a marriage of for you, and from what I have heard in this conversation, this wedding is not one. As hard as it might be for me, I will have to not participate in it," Said her mother

Ted who had never spoke his mind stood up and said:

"Mom, dad, I'm sorry but I must disagree with you two. Dina is getting married, and instead of supporting her, you guys are just judging her. The truth is you were going to be against her wedding anyway."

"You know that's not true Ted", argued his mother.

"It's true mom. First, you advised Dina to not get married to that guy that you did not like because in your opinion he is an "arrogant person" who happens to be white. And then, Dina became the main reason why she should not marry him because she is being honest by telling you how she really feels right now. You are her parents, not her judge, jeez! Right now, she really needs her parents' support and you two just turned your back on her, and you wonder how she became such a cold person?" Maintained Ted

Turning to Dina, he added: "I want to play an active part at your wedding, sis, just tell me how I can help."

"Thanks Ted, but I think the wedding is off now. I don't want to get married without the presence of my parents." Replied Dina

"Okay," said Ted, "can I speak to you privately?

Dina agrees, and followed Ted on the veranda.

"What was that, you want to call off your wedding? Come on Dina, I know that you are eager to leave our parental abode as much as I do. This is a great opportunity for you to do so, don't let mom and dad spoil it for you. They always say that they want us to graduate college, get a job, get married, and fly with our own wings. That is exactly what you have been doing so far Dina, so don't let them discourage you. If they decide to not support you on your wedding day, that's on them, not you. I will suggest that you go ahead with your wedding and prove them that they were wrong for not trusting you." Said Ted

"You're right, I'm going to get married to Derrick, and get out of this house," said Dina, determined.

Chapter 16

Derrick and Dina continued to prepare their wedding. They decided that the ceremony will be held at the Christian Church where Dina and her family are members.

A few months before the wedding ceremony, Dina sat down with her parents' and explained to them that she was still getting married to Derrick and did not need their approval to do so.

"It looks like you are determined to go through with this wedding." Said her mother

"Yes mom, I am, and I know that I should not expect you and dad to come to support me on this special occasion." Responded Dina

"Don't say that baby, your father and I had discussed about it, and we have decided that even if we do not agree with your decision to proceed with this wedding, as your parent's, we must be present at the ceremony to support you." Replied her mother

Dina was overjoyed, she could not believe that her parents had changed their mind, and that they will be attending her wedding ceremony and to assist her.

"Thank you, mom, I really appreciate it." Said Dina.

"You're welcome baby." Replied her mother.

Six weeks later, Derrick and Dina exchanged their vows. It was a small wedding, only family members and close friends were invited. Surprisingly, Derrick's parents were also present. Dina contacted Miranda and invited her to the wedding.

"I can't believe that you are marrying that jerk after what he had put you through. But if you can forgive him, as your friend, I respect your choice," said Miranda.

"Thanks Miranda, I really appreciate your support," said Dina.

Gavin was also invited to the wedding, but he didn't show up. Instead, he sent them a present with a congratulations card.

After the ceremony, Dina and Derrick went to Florida for their honeymoon. When they came back, Dina left her parent's house, and went to live with him in his condo.

"Congratulations Mrs. Lee, I heard that it was a beautiful ceremony," said Gavin, when Dina went back to work after her honeymoon.

"Thank you, but please call me Dina." She replied.

Two months later, Dina who always woke up early to prepare breakfast for Derrick before going together to the office, did not feel like getting out of the bed. She was feeling light headed and tired. She forced herself to get out of the bed, made sandwiches and coffee, and went to prepare herself for work. When she arrived at the office, she ran to the bathroom to pee, and then, started to do her duties.

"There are more charts on my desk," said Doctor Lawrence. "Would you please take them and ask Edna to call the pharmacy and order the medications for the patients, so they can be ready when they go to pick them up?"

"Give me one minute, I must go quickly to the restroom," replied Dina.

"Something is wrong with Dina," thought Gavin, "since the week started; he observed that she kept on going to the bathroom regularly. I know there has been a lot of change in her life, but it's not normal to go to the bathroom that often."

Once Dina came back from the restroom, Gavin went to see her

"Dina, can I talk to you for a minute?" Gavin asked

"Sure, is everything okay?" she asked, since he seemed anxious.

"I am ok, but I'm worried about you, it is not like you to go to the restroom every half hour, but lately, I observe that you must rush to the restroom a lot." Said Gavin

"Oh yeah," realized Dina, "even at night, I feel the need to wake up a few times than usual to go to pee. Maybe I should drink less water."

"No, what you should do is to see a Doctor immediately. I know Derrick can examine you but do not hesitate to come to me if you need any medical advice. Does it burn you when you urinate?" Asked Gavin

"No, but the urgency is really unpleasant. What do you think might cause me to pee as often as I do now?" Enquired Dina

"Well, it can be anything: diabetes, infection, pregnancy...; but since you are a married woman now, the only one that seems plausible is the pregnancy." Said Gavin

"Me, pregnant? No..." replied Dina

"Well, can I at least run a pregnancy test for you, so you can confirm whether you are pregnant or not, it will just take a few minutes as you know; do you want to?" Said Gavin

"Sure, but you are wasting your time Doctor Lawrence, I know that I'm not pregnant." Replied Dina

"Okay, let just run the test so you can eliminate pregnancy from the list," Said Gavin

Gavin told Dina to get a plastic container, and a cotton swab.

"You already know the steps," he said, put at least half of your pee in the plastic container, and pass the applicator in your genital area. It's the same procedure that we explained to the patients, the only difference is that today, I will be the one running the test." Said Gavin

Dina followed Gavin's instruction, and left the jar in the restroom. Gavin went to pick it up and went to the lab section with it.

"I have the result for you Dina," said Gavin.

"So, am I having twins?" Joked Dina, unaware that she was indeed pregnant.

"We don't know yet if you are having twins, but it's confirmed, you are pregnant." Announced Gavin.

Dina was so shocked that she almost fell almost.

"That's... that's impossible..." stammered Dina

"It's not impossible at all Dina; do I have to remind you that you are a married woman now?" said Gavin

"Yes, but... but..." contended Dina

"But what?" Asked Gavin, "you though that you were infertile?" He questioned

"No, but... I took all the precautions," replied Dina

"Well, somehow, you went reckless, and you are pregnant now," explained Gavin

Dina closed her eyes, turned her head from one side to the other and said: "no, no I am always careful... I just don't understand how...."

"Anyway, now we know that your frequent urge to pee is due to your first trimester of pregnancy. The same situation might come back when you're in your last trimester. I will recommend that you start taking prenatal vitamins." Said Gavin

"Seems like you will need a new medical assistant," said Dina ironically

"I can accommodate." Said Gavin. "Besides, it's against the law to get rid of an employee just because she's pregnant," he explained with a smile.

"Well, it's good to know that at least I still have my job," joked Dina

"I will let you go now to announce to your husband this good news, and... congratulations!" Said Gavin

Dina left and went to fix the examination rooms. She was confused and angry she knew that she took all the precautions to keep that from happening, how could this happen? She and Derrick were still struggling with issues on their relationship and were not ready for a baby.

Gavin was very sad, Dina was going to have a child with Derrick. "What was I thinking? that Dina would get tired of him, file for divorce, and marry me? They live together, it was just a matter of time before a baby arrived. There goes my hope to ever marry her! Anyway, something is not right, she seemed to be mad about this pregnancy," thought Derrick

Gavin was still trying to figure out why Dina was not happy about her pregnancy when Derrick abruptly entered his office...

"What did you tell my wife? She seemed very upset and won't even talk to me." Said Derrick.

"I don't have anything to do with her behavior towards you Gavin; all I did was give her the test results." Explained Gavin

"Test result? Since when are you her Doctor? What test result are you talking about, anyway?" asked Derrick

"A pregnancy test result that I ran for her as a complimentary, I thought that both of you would expect to be parents any time, now that you're married, but your wife seemed to be surprised, what happened? Did you rape her, Derrick?" Asked Gavin

"It's ridiculous! She's my wife, how could I rape her." Replied Derrick.

"Well, legally speaking, if you forced her to have sexual relation with you, even though she's your wife, it's called rape Derrick. If it is the case, as you know it, I am required by law to report it to the authorities." Said Gavin

"I didn't rape my wife, okay, she was playing a game with me and I won. She thought she could keep me from having a baby with her. But last month, I discovered that she loves to enjoy a glass of wine from time to time, I just encouraged her to drink a little more. She was not lucid enough to prevent this pregnancy. So, I did not rape her, I just beat her at her own game." Replied Derrick

"That's better, because if it was a rape, even though she's your wife, as I said, I would be required to report it. But why would you play your wife to have a child with her when you know she did not want to." Said Gavin

"She was about to leave me. I overheard her talking to her brother, complotting to escape. She wants to move out of our house; they even started looking for an apartment. Worse, I found a business card of a divorce lawyer inside her purse." Replied Derrick

"And you think that she is not going to leave you now because she's pregnant?" Asked Gavin

"You bet! I know Dina, she doesn't like complicated situations. She would not divorce me knowing that I could take our child away." Replied Derrick

"You would not do such a cruel thing, right Derrick?" Asked Gavin, surprised

"If she tries to leave me, I will. I know you are her confident, so transmitted it to her." Said Derrick. "Look who is worried now, I told you that one day you would be the one worrying about what I could do to her, remember?" He asked before leaving Gavin's office.

The following morning, Dina was feeling nauseous, and light headed. She went to her husband to let him know that she will meet him later one at the office.

"I don't feel good," said Dina; "I think I will be late at work today, you can go, I will rejoin you later?" she added. Derrick agreed, took his prepared lunch, and left.

Every day, Dina and Derrick always go to work together. It was two weeks since she learned that she was pregnant. She wanted to stay at home a little bit, to think about all the events that were taking place in her life.

From the time when, standing behind Gavin's door, she heard Derrick menacing to take away her baby, she was thinking about what to do, how to get away from him and his malicious plan…

"Doctor Lee, your mother in law just called, it's your wife… she's in the emergency room," announced Edna.

"What? Which hospital?" Asked Derrick.

"The Seraph Hospital" Replied Edna.

"Did she said what happened to her," he asked, "she told me that she was not feeling good before I left this morning." He added.

"I don't know, her mother seemed to be in a hurry, so I did not have time to ask her any further questions." Explain Edna

"Let me go to the hospital for you Derrick, you seem really in shock, I don't think it is prudent for you to drive." Proposed Gavin

"Don't worry, I will be okay" assured Derrick, "Dina is *my* wife, so I'm the one who is supposed to be by her side." he added

"Call us as soon as you get there to let us know how she's doing," Said Gavin

When Derrick arrived at the emergency, he learned that Dina was already discharged from the hospital.

"I came as soon as I received the call, how come you had already discharged her?" asked Derrick to the medical staff.

"She said that she was not in pain anymore and the bleeding had stopped. She was mad about the miscarriage, she said that her husband will be mad at her for what happened. She left with her mother." Replied one of the nurses

"She had a miscarriage? That's awful!" Said Derrick

Immediately, Derrick called Dina's mother to know where they were.

"She's in my house, I think it is better for her to stay here for a few days, to recover after what she's been through, she's scared of how you are going to react." Said her mother

"Can I talk to her?" Asked Derrick

"I'm sorry but she doesn't want to talk to you…right now" Replied her mother

"Well, I will call back later, tell her to get some rest and that I love her. All I'm hoping for, is that she will come home soon." Said Derrick

Derrick went back to the hospital, and, thanks to one of the Doctors who is a friend of him, he had access to Dina's emergency room report: *"Patient is a female who is pregnant and fell off the stairs a few hours ago,"* was written on the report.

"So, she fell off the stairs, and that's how it happened," realized Derrick. "I should have stayed with her this morning, when she told me that she did not feel good."

After the office closed, Derrick went to her parents' house, but they did not let him get in her room to see her. He went back home and called her, but only her mother talked to him. The same scenario reproduced the following week. Derrick understood that Dina needed time and space to heal from the miscarriage, so he resolved to do not brusque her. When he called, he contended to talk to his mother in law to enquire from her.

Two weeks later, while Derrick was waiting for Dina to come back home, all he was served with were the divorce papers from her lawyer.

Surprised, Derrick tried to find her to convince her that he was not mad at her for what happened with the pregnancy, but Dina was nowhere to be found and her family refused to disclose to him where she was. He kept the divorce papers without signing them.

"Tell Dina if she wants me to sign the divorce papers, she will have to come to see me, so we can talk about it first," Said Derrick to Dina's parents.

Chapter 17

Dina brought a one-way ticket and traveled to Haiti, her native country. Once at the Aeroport International Toussaint Louverture, Haiti's main airport, she claimed her baggage, and borrowed a mobile phone to call a private transportation company to pick her up. She had to talk louder because there was so much noise at the airport generated by the suitcase's reverberation, and the announcement's commotion.

The day after Dina arrived, she went for a walk in her new neighborhood. While walking on the street, she saw a group of foreigners administrating vaccines to people.

"No wonder we have all those sicknesses" thought Dina. "Any group of people can just land in the country and start to give injections to pregnant women and children, without getting through any background checks whatsoever."

A female vendor was walking on the street carrying a basket on her head and yelling: *"ze bouyi, fig mi."* Being raised in a Haitian household, Dina understood that she was selling "eggs and bananas."

Dina stopped the food vendor and brought a boiled egg and a banana. She handed her a $20 bill and was waiting for her change. The vendor explained to Dina that she didn't have any change yet, as Dina was her first client of the day.

With her limited Kreyol, Dina told the vendor that she could keep the change. There was a surprised look on the vendor's face when she perceived Dina's accent. She smiled and thanked Dina. Then, she took her basket, placed it back on her head and left. Dina realized that Haiti was in fact one of the rare countries where immigrants from all over the world were the most welcome.

When Dina was coming to Haiti, her parents, knowing that she had planned to open some businesses, told her to not get in any car dealer, super market, or gas station businesses, because apparently, these kinds of industries were reserved for the *"lelit"* community, which means *privileged* people. It consists of people from a far geographic area, that immigrated in Haiti between the years of 1880 and 1890, and since then, had kept exclusivity of Haiti's trade, taking it in hostage.

This *"lelit"* people often give a rough ride to native Haitian that tried to diminish their power over the economy.

Dina, who grew up in the democratic states, could not understand how a country could let a group of foreigners take their trade industries in hostage.

"Oh, that's more complicated than you think," said her mother. "In the past, when the Haitian government tried to stop them, they had the back-up of some powerful countries."

Dina learned that most of the young professionals were leaving the country to immigrate somewhere else. It was easier for them to find a job and get on their feet in foreign countries than it was here. But for those who did not have any skills, the struggle was exhausting. They fled Haiti to travel to other countries with the hope of living a better life. Unfortunately, humiliation, dehumanization, and fear of deportation were the biggest part of their everyday lives, while these mercenaries were freely managing Haiti's economy without giving anything back to the community.

Although Dina did not like to disobey her parents, she thought that it was not right for every citizen to cross their arms and let the country getting sucked by a band of corrupted people who had been there for many generations, but never gave a break to the country.

"I am not going to be intimidated by these mercenaries. I always wanted to open a gas station, and a supermarket, so I'm going to pray to God, and I'm going to open both businesses here in Haiti. one day or another, the people of Haiti will realize that they should not accept the fact that only this group of mercenaries own all the big businesses of the country, which give them access to all the good lands and all the privileges." Thought Dina.

"If only people would generate employ for them here in Haiti. If they could just give the appropriate support to the farmers, to help them save their lands and their farms…. "Thought Dina

Dina was living in Port-Au-Prince where she was born which is also the Capital of Haiti. She rented a modest six rooms house at Delmas and started a school for "analphabet" women. These women were hard working people who didn't have a chance to go to school when they were young. She also added a culinary school and a medical clinic at the same school for them.

Since Dina arrived in Haiti, she did not contact Derrick, she tried to forget about him and their failed marriage. She was focused on building a life for herself and her soon to be born baby, and at the same time, helping her community.

As her belly started to grow, it became difficult for Dina to sleep at night. She could not sleep on her back or on her right side. The only position where she was comfortable to sleep was in her left side. She was always tired, since she had to do her laundry manually as she did not have any washer or even a dryer. She also had to wash her dishes by hands because she could not afford a dishwasher yet.

There was rarely electricity. It was often too hot in her room and she did not have any generator to make the fan work. However, the hardest of all for Dina was the fact that she did not have a car, and had to catch the tap-tap, the Haitian public vehicle, where the rides were often rough, thus dangerous for a pregnant woman.

But Dina was happy to be there, because not only Derrick couldn't take her baby away, but also, she was able to help a lot of people, principally women. They were excited to learn to read, and have a certificate in cooking, but more importantly they were happy to have access to healthcare. However, Dina did not realize the supermarket and gas station project yet.

"I need to take an appointment with the Big Business Bank," thought Dina. She picked up her cell phone and dialed the number that she found in the phone book.

"Big Business Bank, comment puis-je vous aider?" said a woman's voice on the phone.

Dina tried to figure out what she was saying, but all she could understand was the name of the bank, she often heard her parents saying that people were mostly talking French in public office and at school, even though the majority of the population only understood Kreyol. Her parents themselves were more comfortable talking Kreyol as it was the language that they talked when they were really mad at her and Ted. When her parents arrived in the United States, they were so eager to learn English that it was the only language that they talked with their children. As a result, Dina and her brother did not learn to talk French.

But, apparently, this language was a big deal in Haiti. People used it to show their peers that they were highly educated.

"Allo," repeated the voice at the end of the other line

"Hello," said Dina. "Mwen rele Dina, mwen pa pale franse, eske ou pale kreyol osinon Angle?" Asked Dina.

"I speak English," answered the woman with a proud tone in her voice.

"Good," replied Dina. My name is Dina Joseph; I need an appointment with the person responsible of project finance.

"Can I know what kind of project it is about?" Asked the woman

"I'm interested in constructing a gas station in the national number one road," explained Dina

"Oh, finally someone with a native Haitian's name who's not scared to enter the big business," express the lady

"Well, I'm just trying..." Said Dina

"Yeah, but that's really courageous of you. Most people are too afraid of these pillagers to participate in that kind of business.

"That's what I learned," is that such a risk? Asked Dina

"Unfortunately, kidnapping and killing are the fate reserved to the few people that had tried in the past. But, if you are prudent, and if you don't go to do money transactions in bad neighborhoods, you don't have anything to worry about." Replied the lady

"Well, thank you for the advice. It would be great if I could make an appointment with a loan officer as soon as possible." Said Dina

"The only available slot that I have is Friday morning at 10:00, is that a good time for you?" she asked

"It's perfect; I will be there around 9:40 a.m." Replied Dina.

"What is your last name again?" Asked the lady.

"It's Joseph Lee, and it's spelled: J-o-s-e-p-h, L-e-e." Spelled Dina

"And your first name is:" asked the lady.

"Dina: D-I-N-A." Said Dina.

"Do you have any phone number where we can reach you?" The lady asked.

"Sure, the number is: 304-77-77." Said Dina.

"Do you have any detailed plan about your project?" Asked the lady.

"Yes, I do…" Replied Dina.

"It would be a good idea to bring a copy." Said the lady.

"Okay, I will bring a copy of it then. Are there any other documents that I should bring?" asked Dina.

"Another one is your Identification National Card, I know you will have it on you as you were living abroad, and it's the first document people ask every time you go to a public place." Said the lady

"That's true, you should not leave your house without your identification card or any other form of identification." Agreed Dina.

"Yeah, do you know where we are located?" Asked the lady.

"Not really, I was going to ask you for the direction," Replied Dina.

"Can you receive text message from the phone number that you just provide to me?" enquired the lady.

"Yes, it's a smart phone." Said Dina.

"Great, I'm going to send you the direction via a text message." The lady said.

"Well, thank you very much," replied Dina.

"You are welcome, have a nice day!" she said.

"You too, thank you."" Said Dina.

On Friday morning, at 10:00 a.m. exactly, Dina arrived at the bank. She told one of the security guards that she was there to see a loan officer, and he told her that she needed to get an appointment first. Dina explained to him that she already set up an appointment, and that's why she was there today.

The security showed her a register and told her to go there to talk to one of the associates. Dina went to the register and explained to one of the associates the reason of her visit. He asked to see her identification, she showed it to him, then he picked up a phone and pressed an extension. He talked in French with someone, and after he hang up the phone, he told her to be patient, and that someone was coming to talk to her. After more than twenty minutes, an elegant light skin woman came from behind a close door, and introduced herself to Dina, then, he asked Dina to follow her in a room, where at least six people where sharing. She indicated a chair to her to sit, and she sat on it.

"How are you today Mrs. Lee?" Said the loan officer.

"I'm good thank you," replied Dina.

"I understand that you are interested in opening a gas station in our community." Said the loan officer.

"Yes, I already have the land and a few equipment's, I need a loan to finish with the construction and order the fuel." Explained Dina.

"Unfortunately, we are unable to borrow you the money at this time." Said the loan officer.

"Well, do you know when I can check back with the bank?" Asked Dina.

"Mrs. Lee, you were born here, right?" She asked.

"Yes," replied Dina.

"So, you know perfectly how it works. The banks here have a well determined group of people that they lend money to. If your maiden name is Joseph, or Jean, like mine, and are not part of their inner circle, we don't stand any chance." Said the loan officer.

"Really? Well, that's not fair, I thought that, as the loan officer, you were the one making the decision" replied Dina

"I know, but I am just an employee here, and I have to follow their guidelines, I hope that you understand," said the loan officer

"Yes, I get it, well, thank you for your time," replied Dina, while standing

"Here, call the number on this card, talk to them, maybe they will be able to help you" said the loan officer

"Thank you, bye." Replied Dina

"Have a nice day." Added the loan officer

Dina could not believe the way that those lenders were treating the Haitian population. She always heard about it, but thought they were just rumors, that it couldn't possibly be true, but now, she had the proof.

"My parents were right about the kind of business that the population can start in Haiti. At least, I have the school and the clinic to keep me busy." Thought Dina.

Dina's parents, and her brother Ted often called her to enquire to her health. Her mother was making plans to come to visit her with her father. Dina learned that her brother Ted is now a father of two, since Angel gave birth to twin boys. Ted had found a job as a mailman and is able to provide for his children. The only problem was with Angel; Dina's mother told her that Angel wanted Ted to move back with him. But because Ted refused, Angel banned him from seeing his twins. She claimed that since Ted and her are not married, and that Ted's name is not on the birth certificates of the twins, he has no legitimate status that gives him the right to see his kids.

Moved by the way that not being able to see his boys has affected Ted, Dina's parent contacted a lawyer, who told them that, to share custody of his children with Angel, Ted would have to take a DNA test to determine his paternal standing. After witnessing the way that Angel treated Ted at her house, Dina thought that he took a good decision by refusing to go back to leave with Angel, but she felt sorry for him that he was not allowed to see his own kids.

Months past and Dina's belly was getting bigger. One night, while she was sleeping, she felt that she needed to urinate. She went to the bathroom and after she finished to pee, she realized that she was still leaking. Dina did not know what to think, so she woke up one of her employees who told her that it was her water breaking, and that her baby was on its way.

Dina called one of the Doctors that worked at the medical clinic for advice and he told her to go to the nearest hospital which has multiple medical staff and better equipment. As soon as Dina arrived at the hospital, they admitted her, and gave her a room. A nurse came and changed her clothes against a hospital gown, wrapped a pair of belts around Dina's belly to monitor her baby's heart rate and measure her contractions. Then, the nurse took a swab and take a sample of her amniotic fluid; we are going to run a test to confirm that it is your water that is broken.

Hours had passed and yet, Dina did not feel any ache. "Whoever said that giving birth was painful; I still don't feel any pain," thought Dina.

A few minutes later, Dina was looking at the windows and saw the nurses and the Doctors talking while looking at her room. One of the Doctors came to her room and inform her that, since her water was previously broken, and that her cervix was not widening, she must have a C-section immediately to save her baby. The same nurse that was checking the baby's heart rate came back, and shaved Dina's pubic hair., Soon after, an anesthesiologist came, asked Dina to sit on the bed and informed her that since it is a delicate procedure, she must not move while he is administrating her the anesthesia medication.

Dina layed awake on the bed, and they placed a curtain to keep her from seeing the operation. When Dina heard her baby cry, she felt an immense joy. It's a boy, said one of the Doctors. Dina wanted to see her baby right away, but the Doctor handed the baby to a nurse to get him clean. After they were done with the surgery, they placed a catheter into Dina's bladder. Four days later, they removed the intravenous lines that they had placed in her vein, and the catheter as well. A nurse told Dina that it was time for her to try to walk.

The nurse helped Dina to get out of the bed. Dina stood up, and walked slowly to the bathroom, she stood in front of the large mirror, and discovered that she has a horizontal scar near her pubic hairline.

Chapter 18

Three years later, Dina was in her room, feeding her son and making him sleep, when Nadine, one of the employees knocked at her door, and informed her that a white man who said his name was "*Gavein Lorence*," was outside, and wanted to talk to her.

Dina was surprised, the only white man she knew whose name sounds like that was Gavin Lawrence. She knew that Gavin was all the way in the States and could not possibly be in Haiti. She took the bottle of milk out of her son's mouth, put him on the bed, and covered him with a blanket. Then, she went to the window, opened the curtain and looked at the house entrance; Gavin was indeed standing there, a backpack on his shoulders, and a luggage in his hand.

Dina could not believe it. "I must be dreaming! How in the world did Gavin get my address, and why is he here?" She thought, she didn't know what to do.

After further thinking, she decided to see him

"You can let him in, give him a seat in the common room. I will join him shortly." She said to Nadine.

Dina washed her face and applied a light make up on. She sprayed a little bit of perfume on herself. Then, she called Nadine and asked her to stay in her room to watch her son while she was talking to Gavin.

"Doctor Lawrence, what a wonderful surprise. To what do I owe this visit from you?" Asked Dina

"I'm doing good, thank you," said Gavin, ironically, "What about you, Dina?"

"I'm sorry if I sounded rude, it was not my intention. I was just wondering what happy occasion had brought you here, in Haiti; it is so far from Maryland. Are you on vacation?" Asked Dina

"I need to talk to you, privately, Dina" Said Gavin

"I'm sorry but this is the only place where I can have a conversation with you," replied Dina

"What about the room where you have left your son?" declared Gavin

Did he just say my son? No, it can't be true, he wouldn't know... Thought Dina

"My son? how did you know about him?" Asked Dina

"It's not what is important, Dina, I really need to talk to you in private." Said Gavin

Convinced, Dina invited him to follow her

"That way," indicated Dina.

She went to her room with Gavin, thanked Nadine for watching her son, and told her that she could leave.

"What do you want from me, Gavin?" Asked Dina nervously

"I just want you to stop running. You ran away from the university and abandoned your dream of becoming a lawyer. Then, two years later you ran away again, leaving behind you your family, your friends and your job. Worse, this time you left behind an angry husband and now you are keeping a child from seeing his father. Why can't you just stop running?" Replied Gavin

"Because I didn't want to live with him anymore." Said Dina

"Then, you should just get a divorce, Dina, that's what rational people do, they don't fake a miscarriage and disappear." Replied Gavin

"That's what I did, but he never signed the papers. If I had stayed there, waiting for him to sign the divorce papers, he would have taken away my baby as he had planned to. He knew I didn't want to get pregnant right away, why do you think he played me and made it happen anyway?" Said Dina

"However, you shouldn't take away his son, Dina." Replied Gavin

"Technically, I didn't take away his son; I was still pregnant when I left." Said Dina

"But you have misled him by making him think that you had a miscarriage. What do you think he's going to do when he finally finds you?" Said Gavin

"He will not find me" I've been hiding here for three years." Replied Dina

"How can you be so sure? I have found you, so can he." Explained Gavin

"How did you find me?" Asked Dina

"Your family told me where to find you." Replied Gavin

"I cannot believe that my family disclosed my location to you." Said Dina

"They gave me your address only after I told them everything that I learned from an investigator that Derrick hired. He called Derrick to inform him that he found you, and that you had a mixed child; fortunately, we have a new medical assistant working at the reception, she mistakenly forwarded the message to me instead of Derrick." Replied Gavin

Dina was in shock, she didn't know that Derrick had hired a private investigator to find her.

"Do you think that Derrick will find me?" Asked Dina

"It's just a matter of time, Dina. In the message that he had left, the investigator said he has recent pictures of you that he wanted to show to Derrick as proof. As we speak, he might have already contacted Derrick to give him the pictures and to withdraw his check." Said Gavin.

Immediately, Dina pulled the blanket away, and woke up her son.

"What are you doing?" Asked Gavin

"I'm leaving this house, I'm not going to sit here and wait for Derrick to take my son away from me." Said Dina

"No, this time, I won't let you run away, and abandoned everything you have built here, Dina. I chatted with the taxi driver who drove me to your address, and he told me how helpful you were for this community. You have opened your house to teach women who did not have the chance to go to school how to read, you have equipped them with culinary certificate, so they can go ahead and make a life for themselves, you have provided a low-cost clinic for them, so they could see a Doctor when they need one. If you close this establishment, these people are going to be affected by it." Replied Gavin

"I refuse to sit here and wait for Derrick to take control of my life again!" Yelled Dina

"Then, stop running, stay and fight. Better yet, ask a qualified person to take charge of your house, and go back to the States to face Derrick legally. This is the only way that you can keep him from gaining control of your life again." Said Gavin.

Dina laugh hysterically.

"Is that a joke or what? Do you really want me to go back and face him legally? You know I don't stand a chance. Just visualize the picture: a poor immigrant black woman, versus a rich white guy, who happened to be a Doctor on top of it. If I do that, he would have custody of my son before he even snaps his fingers." She replied

"You won't be alone Dina; I will be at your side in every step of this, I promise." Said Gavin

"Thanks, but I prefer to follow my instinct." Maintained Dina

"And what does your instinct tell you, Dina?" Asked Gavin

"That I should take my son and go to another city, where his investigator would not be able to locate me." Said Dina

"There's no such place, this country is occupied, I know that people call it "mission of stabilization," but you and I know perfectly that just a fancy name for a peaceful transnational occupation. I learned from a trusted source that this investigator was previously deployed here. He knows people that know people, he would probably locate you just a few days after you arrived anywhere else." Explained Gavin

Dina sat down with her son in her arms and started crying. Gavin rejoined her and put his arms around them. He pressed his head towards hers, to comfort her. For a moment, Dina felt so good and protected. When Gavin pulled away, Dina looked at him, he appeared worried.

"If I go back to the States, do you really think I can win this?" Asked Dina

"I cannot promise you that Derrick will not be allowed to share custody of his son with you, but I promise you that I won't let him take him away from you. Trust me, it's the only way to keep him peacefully out of your life. Do you want to give it a shot?" Replied Gavin

"And if things don't work as expected?" Said Dina

"Well, I have already contacted one of my lawyers; he will be at the airport waiting for us at our arrival." He explained to me that we might have other options."

"We?" said Dina surprised, "who are you talking about"

"I'm talking about us, you and me. I told you that you weren't alone in this situation, Dina." Replied Gavin

"So, what are the other options? Asked Dina

"We will have more details about them later, but one of the options that my lawyer had suggested to me was to marry you as soon as possible, but given that you did not divorce Derrick yet, it's practically off the table. Unless..." started Gavin

"Unless what?" Asked Dina

"Unless you accelerate the divorce process before he finds you. My lawyer can start working on it as soon as we land, which means you should start packing right now."

Seeing that Dina was not moving, and was looking at him incredibly, Gavin added:

"Look, if you don't trust me, you don't have to come back. But if you really believe that I'm devoted to help you keep your son and stop running from Derrick, start packing right now, and be ready to show him that he no longer has control over your life, and that you are really over him."

"Oh, I wasn't thinking about Derrick, I was just wandering why you are doing all of this for me." Asked Dina

"To tell the truth, I don't even know the answer myself, is that bad?" Replied Gavin

"No, it's not bad, it's not bad at all..." Replied Dina.

They stared into each other's eyes for a few seconds, without saying a word. Finally, Gavin approached Dina, leaned his face near hers, and they kissed.

Dina felt like she was in another world and wanted to stay like this as much as possible. Instinctively, she closed her eyes were instinctively closed. She could feel her heartbeat accelerate, "wow, I never felt like that before, I am in love with Gavin, I am so in love with him…" thought Dina

When they finally stepped back out of the kiss, Dina handed her son to Gavin, and started packing the things that she needed for the voyage. The sweet kiss they had exchanged gave her full confidence in Gavin…

"Just take the essentials of what you need, we will buy more clothes once we arrived in the States".

"Okay," replied Dina

She took one of her suitcases, threw a pack of her son's diapers, and two changing clothes for her and her baby. She also took her make-up kit and grabbed their passports.

While Dina was packing, Gavin profited to look closely at the little boy that he was holding. "He looks exactly like Derrick," he taught, the only difference was the skin color, Derrick was completely white, while his son was turning pink. He just wished that this child was from him and Dina, not from Derrick and her. He felt ashamed to feel that way.

After Dina finished, they went to Carrefour-feuille at the Hotel were Gavin was staying. Once there, Gavin went online, and brought the tickets, then he contacted his lawyer, and informed him of their arrival for the day after.

In the morning, Gavin's cell phone rang, thinking that it was his lawyer contacting him, Gavin answered:

"Hello," Said Gavin

"Where is my wife, Gavin, I want to talk to her?" Said Derrick

Realizing that was Derrick's voice, Gavin put the speaker on.

"I don't know what you are talking about," lied Gavin.

"Indeed, you perfectly know. I will tell you what I know instead then: I know that you are trying to help a woman that kidnapped my son and escaped. She will be arrested at the airport while you two will be landing here," threatened Derrick

Seeing that Gavin wasn't answering him, he continued:

"What happened Gavin, have you lost your tongue. You remember what I told you that could potentially happen: I told you I would marry Dina, and that one day you will be the one worried about what I could do to her. It's the second time that I feel that you worried about what I could do to her. I think this day is near were you will witness what I will do to her. None of this would ever happen if you didn't continue to pursue her after we got married. I warned you, but you weren't listening, you just wanted to have the woman that I had, while you could have had many others." Said derrick

"If you are after me, then leave Dina alone. I will do whatever you ask me to, if you spare her." Replied Gavin

"No, no, no, it would be too easy for her, she's not innocent in all of this, she encouraged you. The only deal that would work for her would be to come back home with my son, and reunify the family that she broke, otherwise, she will go to jail and I would have sole custody of my son. Where is she, put her on the phone." Yelled Derrick

"Calm down Derrick, okay, she doesn't want to talk to you, but you and I are longtime friends, we can work this out." Said Gavin

"From now on, I don't want anything to do with you, Gavin. I just want to see my wife and my son. As for our friendship, it's dead to me." Replied Derrick

"Well I was just trying to help you work things out with Dina, so she could let you see your son. But if you don't want me to…, I won't insist, if she's not in the States, you cannot touch her." Said Gavin

"Really, that's what you think? For someone who is in love with a Haitian immigrant, you seemed not well informed about her third world country. Let me just bring to your attention that we have the right to go to Haiti and arrest anybody at any time, including your kidnapper lover. You might think "how in the world is that possible?" Well, one of their anti-patriotic and greedy presidents signed this pact several years ago. So, I don't need your help to get my son back. The only thing you can do is to ask her to surrender." Replied Derrick

"Surrender? Are you out of your mind Derrick? She's not wanted for anything as far as I know." Said Gavin

"Not yet, but my lawyers are working closely with the child protective services to see how we can bring my son back and arrest his kidnapper. You know Lewis, he never liked Dina, and it's a real pleasure for him to hunt her down." Explained Derrick

"Unbelievable, you teamed up with someone who hates your wife to make her life miserable. Why don't you just sign the divorce papers, and give that woman her freedom?" Asked Gavin

"She teamed up with someone I thought was my best friend to keep my son away from me, and it doesn't seem being a problem for you," replied Derrick.

"She did not team up with me against you, okay, I didn't even know that she had a son until this week. I bet she couldn't take it anymore with your arrogance and your infidelity, and that's why she left you." Said Gavin.

"You know what I think, Gavin? I think that Dina is the queen of cheaters now. Legally, she's still my wife and she is currently in a hotel room with you, don't you think it is being a hypocrite talking about my infidelity?" Replied Derrick

"Nothing had happened between Dina and I, I guarantee you," affirmed Gavin

"Oh, come on, do you really expect me to believe that? I saw the way you looked at her at the office. And many times, she called me *Gavin* while we were together. I know that you two wanted to be together, but she had the choice, and she married me, she should respect her vow. I will show her what it cost to be disloyal to me." Said Derrick

"She knows how painful it is to have been betrayed, Gavin, you dumped her once, remember? She could have divorced you without your signature on the papers as you were served with the divorce petition. Why do you think she didn't stay and request a default divorce? Asked Gavin

"I bet you are going to tell me," Replied Derrick

"That's because she knew that you were hurt, she didn't want to make it worse by asking the courts for a final hearing to go on with the divorce. I warned you that she was marrying you just to avenge your betrayal, but you didn't want to listen to me. Now, I'm imploring you, give Dina her freedom, so you and her can work out your differences, and focus in your son's future. Do you think your son will ever forgive you for putting his mother in jail? He will hate you for that and trust me, that would be the worst thing that could happen to you." Said Gavin

"Just ask her that if I move out of the house, if she's willing to come back." Asked Derrick

"She's ready to share custody of your son with you, but not to go back in your life as your wife Derrick." Replied Gavin

"And who decided it like that," asked Derrick

"Dina did," Said Gavin

"No, she didn't, I know that she didn't, you did, Gavin," argued Derrick

"She's stronger than you think, Derrick, and she's smarter than you might suspected." Replied Gavin

"If it's true, she would pick up the phone, and tell me that herself, she would not use a manipulator like you to do it for her." Maintained Derrick

Immediately, Dina grabbed the phone from Gavin and stated:

"You and I are over Derrick, but for the best interest of Ethan, I will come back, and I will share his custody with you, but besides that, I don't want anything to do with you."

"So, when are you coming." Asked Derrick

"As soon as I receive a signed paper from your lawyers guaranteeing me that I won't be charged for leaving with my son." Said Dina

"Well, I will contact my lawyers and see what we can do about it." Replied Derrick

"Perfect; just send me a copy of it, whenever you're ready. I can wait another year... or more here. Better yet, I might have time to divorce you and marry Gavin by the time you find me; he would be such a good stepfather for your son. Kids are like glue you know, they possess the ability to stick very well to the person that fulfill their emotional and material comfort. Maybe this is the way it must be, who knows." Said Dina

"Do you really think Gavin will stay in your shithole country just to live with you? His parents and his business are here. As soon as he finishes his "affair" with you, he will leave you all alone, and will come back to his usual fancy life. This is the way it's going to be, and you'll be all alone and scared, and angry. This is the moment where I will let my lawyers dispose of you, all that I will care about is my son, so now that you have the possibility, just come back, and I will forgive you. This is the only guaranty that I can give you." Replied Derrick

Gavin intervened and said:

"Wow, you really don't know the extent of what you did a few years ago when you betrayed her. Let me tell you that what you just described was exactly the way that she was the first time I saw her, she was alone, scared, and angry, sitting in a crowded nightclub looking at couples dancing in the podium....I saw this sparkle of hope when I invited her to dance with me, then she wasn't alone anymore. She put her head on my chest and we danced all night long. Then her friends were leaving, and she had to go with them. I asked her for her phone number, and she got scared, scare that I would come in her life and do the same things that you did. Instead of giving me her number she became angry and insulted me, right in front of her friends.... Yes, this is exactly how she was after you left her, that's why I'm not going anywhere without her. I will stay in Haiti with her if she needs me to. Together, we will find a way to resolve the custody issue. I just wish that you weren't that stubborn. I have to go now." Replied Gavin

"Now, you're an accomplice Gavin, so, I will see you in court as well; you know I will find her, there is no place for her to hide in her deserted homeland." Said Derrick.

By the way, you should come to visit her native country, it is not a shithole as you assumed, people there are very welcoming, hardworking and intelligent. You'd be surprised to see how most of them are more civilized and resilient than you are." Replied Gavin

Dina was shaking, not only she risked to lost custody of her son, but also, Derrick was threatening her. Gavin put both of his arms around her to calm her.

"I know things are tough for you right now, but trust me, we will get through this, okay?" Said Gavin.

"Yeah but when? How long is it going to take before I get a break from Derrick?" Asked Dina.

"The only solution that I can think of, for now, is to let him have custody of Ethan, just temporary." Said Gavin

"What?" Shouted Dina incredulously. "I can't believe what you are suggesting me to do. You promise you won't let him take my baby away from me."

"And I intend to keep my promise, Ethan is not going to stay permanently with him, it's just a brief solution that might calm his furor down for a while. In the meantime, you could divorce him, and perhaps get married to me; what do you think?" Asked Gavin

"You want to know what I think? I think that you and Derrick planned this whole saga. You are here to help him against me, admit it Gavin. I am just a black woman at your mercy, right?" Asked Dina

"No, I'm here to help you get your life back, and save what you have built here in your native country, but you are so focused and consumed by those racists and malicious people that you cannot see and appreciate many others that are kind and fair. However, I completely understand your apprehension; just tell me what I can do to prove that you are wrong about me." Said Gavin

"I might be wrong, but you are Derrick's best friend and associate, you have too much to lose in this if you are really on my side. I really don't know what you can do to win my trust." Replied Dina

"I heard you asking Derrick for a signed paper as a warrant of your immunity, maybe you should ask me for one also." Suggested Gavin

"It's not a bad idea, maybe I should." Agreed Dina

"Just tell me word by word what you want me to sign, and I will do it." Affirmed Gavin

"Seriously, you would do that?" Asked Dina

"Of course, I would," confirmed Gavin. "So, tell me what your warranty paper should stipule?"

"Before anything, I think we need to talk, Gavin," Said Dina

"Ok, let us talk, what do you have in mind?" Enquired Gavin

"It's not about what I have in mind, it's about what is obvious, and what is obvious is that I don't know why you want to help me." Said Dina

"I told you, I love you Dina, and I want us to be together, I want you to be my wife." Replied Gavin

"Well, first, I'm already married to Derrick, even if we ever get divorce, I would not be able to marry you because I'm a Christian and I know any second marriage will be considered as adultery. I married Derrick at a Church Gavin, and you know it. Secondly, do you realize that I'm black?" Asked Dina

"Yes, since the first night that I saw you. What is the issue about that?" Replied Gavin

"We need to talk about it. Your family, do you think that they will accept me?" Said Dina

"I see, you're playing the race card now, huh? Have you ever talked about this race thing with Derrick? I bet not. And what does your religion had to do with you and me? You were already a Christian at the university when you and Derrick were hitting it off. And speaking about my family, from what I have heard, you didn't care at all about what Derrick's family thought of you. You are just trying to find a reason to get rid of me. Sorry but these tactics won't work with me." Replied Gavin

"You're right I was already a Christian when I made the mistake to have sex with Derrick before getting married. Since then, I took the resolution to never committed this sin again. And concerning Derrick's family, he told me what to expect from them, which is not the case with you. Anyway, you probably here to help your associate, so I'm going to find a lawyer, and make him write an official document that would allow me to sue you if you ever participate in anything against me that could help Derrick to get full custody of Ethan." Said Dina

"Listen to yourself! suing me for helping Derrick against you!? since when did you become a conspiracy theorist?" Asked Gavin.

"Well, conspiracy theory or not, I need a document that can guarantee me immunity in case my suspicion is right. I just want a paper that state that you convinced me to come back home and that you won't let Derrick take away my son."

"First, Dina, you must understand that Ethan is Derrick's son too. Neither of you should have sole custody of him; you two should just reach a share custody agreement. However, I will offer you a better deal instead, I will sign a warranty paper that state that I will take care of your lawyers' fees as soon as we get to the States if I ever help Derrick against you, deal? He asked

"Deal," confirmed Dina but don't try to play me," she warned. "Now, if you'll excuse me, I have some places to go," said Dina.

"Where?" asked Gavin.

"I'm going to buy two extra pacifiers for Ethan, I need them to keep him from crying during the trip." Replied Dina.

"I want to come with you, I don't want anything to happen to you while you are on the streets. It seems that Derrick has some good connections here." Said Gavin.

"I don't believe he can do anything to me here, this is my hometown after all. I think Derrick was bragging about most of the things that he said. Anyway, you are welcome to accompany me." Replied Dina.

Chapter 19

Dina, accompanied with Gavin, went to the store and brought two pacifiers, and some other items for babies that they had found.

After they left the store, they walked on the street slowly, they saw people selling all kinds of food on the street. It was a hot day, Dina saw a man selling bottles of water, she brought one for herself and one for Gavin. Dina opened her bottle of water and drank some, then, she poured some into her palm and splashed it on her face. In the corner of the street, was a two-story house with a porch. Two little girls were sitting on the floor, playing *"osselets,"* a traditional Haitian game played with five knucklebones of goats. One of the girls, flung a knucklebone in the air, and it landed in one of the four sides. Dina was too far from them to see exactly which side it landed on, but she knew that the face is identified as *do*, the back as *kre,* the straight side as *i*, and the curved side as *s*. They stood there looking at the girls, who were simultaneously throwing up one knucklebone and gathering one or more from the floor while the one they threw up was still in the air, and for a moment, they forgot about all the difficulties that Dina was facing.

As they had a morning flight, Dina and Gavin accompany of Ethan made their way to the gate full of passengers. After boarding the plane, they sat side to side, and shared the arm rests of their seats, and the leg space. Dina felt a frisson every time that their arms and legs touched.

Dina's son Ethan who was placed on a seat near her, slept during the whole flight.

Finally, the plane landed at Miami airport. Gavin called his lawyer who came with his minivan to pick them up. Gavin and his lawyer where at the back of the car chatting and loading the luggage's into the back of the car, and Dina was inside the van fixing her son's car seat when she heard what she perceived as an argument, as she was raising her head to see what was going on, she saw Derrick opening the van's door

I told you that I would find you, said Derrick; now, you're coming with me or I will call the police.

"You better leave, Derrick," argued Gavin." She's tired and your son is sleeping. They are going with me while my lawyer and yours are working on a joint custody."

"That's my family, Gavin; you stay away from this. Come on Dina, if you come with me, I promise I will forgive you for everything." Said Derrick

"Put your seat belt Dina, we're leaving." Replied Gavin

"Don't do that Gavin, if you try to leave with her, I would get her arrested." Threatened Derrick

"No, you can't, right Edmund," asked Gavin to his lawyer

"Can I speak with you for a minute? Replied Edmund

They both went to the front of the car to talk. As they were talking, Dina could see Gavin placing his hands on his waists, and shaking his head in disbelief; then, Gavin turned his head to look at Dina who was still sitting in the car.

"Something is wrong, Gavin looked really sad," observed Dina.

Derrick opened the car seat and took Ethan from it.

"No, you cannot take him with you," exploded Dina,

Rapidly, Dina detached her seatbelt buckle to try to stop Derrick. Gavin immediately walked towards Dina and said:

"Edmund didn't have time to address the kidnapping charge that Derrick had started against you. Let him have Ethan just for today so we can challenge the kidnapping allegation in court as early as tomorrow. After that you will be able to share custody of Ethan with him."

Dina was furious, she couldn't believe that she had just landed, and Derrick was already in control of her life.

"Fine," surrendered Dina, "but please be careful with him, he's a very active little guy."

"Oh, I'm not only leaving with Ethan, you're coming with us as well, Dina; we're not a family without you." Said Derrick.

"It's off the table, Derrick," shouted Gavin. "You already have her son, don't put her through this with you again."

"*Her* son? that's my son too, Gavin, and Dina is still my wife; I don't need your permission to take none of them with me, just ask your lawyer if you don't believe me." Replied Derrick

"You can call the police if you want, I won't come with you," said Dina

"All right, your choice," said Derrick, while starting to type the local emergency number in his phone.

"Wait," shouted Gavin, "what about you let Dina stay at a hotel tonight, she's exhausted," added Gavin

"Only if my son and I can stay with her, as a family" replied Derrick

Gavin was thinking, which one was worse: "Let the woman that I'm in love with stay in a hotel room with Derrick, or let Derrick call the police on her?" He realized that it would be better for Dina to simply stay with Derrick. "It's just for one day, and at least Dina will have her son with her." thought Gavin.

"Is that okay with you Dina?" Asked Gavin

"I don't want to share a room with you, Derrick, you cannot force me to do that" Said Dina, defiantly

"I will take a room with two beds, and I won't touch you, you have my word," replied Derrick

"Your words have no values to me, Derrick, but try to touch me and I will be the one calling the police." Warned Dina

"Let's check The Permanent Hotel, it always has a few unoccupied rooms and they accept walk-ins," proposed Gavin.

"Sure, let's go consented Derrick. My car is parked at the rear of the airport, Gavin can drive you there if you want, let me just borrow your car seat, I will drive my son."

"See you at the hotel," said Derrick to Dina; "do not attempt to do anything stupid that you might regret."

Derrick held his son with his left arm, the car seat with his right hand, and walked towards the rear of the airport to his car. Once there, he installed the car seat at the back seat of his car and placed his son in it. After buckled his son into the car seat, Derrick went behind the wheel, and drove in the direction of The Permanent hotel as planned.

When Derrick arrived, Dina was already there waiting with Gavin and Edmund, his lawyer. Derrick get out the car and opened the back door to grab his son. They walked to the hotel entrance altogether, Derrick was holding Ethan, and Gavin was carrying Dina's luggage. After they checked in, Gavin gave Dina his cell phone to carry, in case she needed to make a call. I will come to check on you early tomorrow. Before leaving, Gavin wrote down his other phone number, then handed it to Dina.

"This is the number that I can be reach; do not hesitate to call me if you need anything." Said Gavin

"Great," said Dina "you took me from my safety place, brought me here, and now, you are just leaving me with Derrick?"

"Listen to me Dina, Derrick is determined to either keep you and his son with him tonight, or got you arrested. I want you to stay at the hotel with your son and play along. If he stays in his own bed as he said he will, it will be a good thing for him. If he tries to take advantage of you, you can file an attempt of rape against him." Said Gavin

"Thanks Gavin, but I don't have time for your heartfelt conversation," said Derrick, "We will take it from here, I'm eager to spend some quality time with my wife and my son."

"Alright, do not hesitate to call me Dina, goodnight." Said Derrick

As soon as Gavin left, he went to the house of Dina's parent to inform them of the situation. Gavin also wrote down the phone number where they could reach Dina. Dina's mother composed the number right after Gavin left to talk to her daughter.

Ethan was awakened while his father was putting him in one of the double beds of their hotel room. Derrick sat on the bed near his son and was just looking at him. Dina and Derrick did not say a word to each other since they entered the room.

Dina was opening her luggage to take a new diaper and a box of wipers to change Ethan when the cell phone that Gavin borrowed her started to vibrate. Thinking that it was Gavin calling already, Dina swiped the answering button and was surprised and happy to hear her mother's voice.

"How are you? and Ethan, how is he? I heard about what Derrick is doing, I'm really sorry that you have to go through this, but don't worry, everything is going to be fine. I'm praying for you, okay?" Said her mother.

"I know mom, I'm sorry too that I had put you and dad through this. How's dad doing?" Asked Dina.

"He's beside me, let me put him on the phone." Replied her mother.

"Hi, dad" Said Dina

"Hi, how are you holding up?" asked her father

"I'm with Ethan, so I'm feeling pretty good now," answered Dina, before bursting into tears.

"Don't cry baby, everything is going to be all right, okay," Replied her father.

"We don't know that, dad, all Derrick wants is to take Ethan away from me." Said Dina.

"According to my source, he also wants you to come to live with him. I hope that you have learned by now, that as parent's, sometimes we must choose what is best for our child." Explained her father.

"I can't believe you dad! you are asking me to go back to live with this man who just want to punish me and is using my child as a pretext to get close to me again." Replied Dina.

"Well, let me remind you that you made that choice, you are the one that chose this man instead of your law degree. Now, it's up to you to allow your son to be raised by both of his parents, or to let your husband raise him without you. You have a brain Dina, use it!" Said her father

"Wow, dad is angry at me more than I thought," sensed Dina. "I better put an end at this conversation to let him cool down."

"I'm sorry that I disappointed you dad. I think that I should go now, it was nice to hear from you and mom," Replied Dina

"That's' right, run, run; every time things get tough for you, instead of fighting back the odds, you run away. Let me just remind you that

136

running away does not solve problems, it solely makes things worse. Sooner or later, you will have to face your challenges." Said her father

"Bye dad, I must go now, talk to you later." replied Dina.

Dina hung up the phone and cried her eyes out. Now, even her own father was against her.

Dina's mother was sitting beside her father, she gave him a disapproving look.

"What?" Questioned her father.

"That was really cold what you just did to your daughter. You should have never talked to her like that." Said her mother.

"All I did was tell her the truth; I'm sorry if I sounded cruel, but you need to realize that she hasn't demonstrated any good judgment lately. For Dina to take better decisions, she needed a good reality check than a pat on her back. We should have told her how we really felt since the day that she came back here without her law degree, maybe then she could have gotten her act together. She's a mother now, she must think about her child first. That's exactly the point that I was trying to make before she managed to hang up the phone." Replied her father.

Dina's mother stood up and left the room without replying to her husband.

Derrick who was listening to the conversation between Dina and her father, said to her:

"I hope you will listen to your father, Dina. All I want now is our son's happiness."

"Me too," admitted Dina.

"So, why can't we just make peace?" He asked

"Because it's not that easy Derrick, things are so complicated between us, you always find a way to jeopardize our relationship." Argued Dina.

"I know, I'm not going to deny that we did have some dark times, but you must admit that, besides of these heartaches, we also had some great times together Dina, right?" Asked Derrick

"Well, what you call great times were actually the most chaotic ones for me. And, I don't even know why you are calling our painful times "dark," because if these times were actually dark, I could have known even a little bit of serenity at that time. Would you just stop calling every negative thing dark? Said Dina

"It's not me, that's the dictionaries' definitions Dina." Replied Derrick.

"Well, undoubtfully, the dictionaries have it wrong. Most of us prefer to sleep in the dark because it's peaceful. Dark is calm, relaxing, it allows people to reflect more on themselves. People still can find their way in the dark; I know that it sounds ridiculous, but ask people that are blind, and they will tell you." Said Dina

"I agree with you," replied Derrick

"Now, if you'll excuse me, I feel sleepy already. I am going to brush my teeth and take a shower." Said Dina.

"Sure, it's good to have you back, you know…" Declared Derrick.

"Well, it's good to see my son finally reunited with his father also. I better go to take that shower before I fall asleep." Replied Dina.

Dina went to the restroom, brushed her teeth, and took a shower. Then, she got on her knees to pray to God, and went to sleep in the empty bed.

"Good night…" whispered Derrick.

"Good night," replied Dina

Gavin could not sleep, he was anxious, frustrated and hopeless, thinking about Dina, and the difficult situation in which she was stuck with Derrick. The alarm that he set off had awakened him. He jumped from his bed, took a quick shower, grabbed his car keys and went to pick up Dina.

While he was on his way, he called Edmund, his lawyer, who told him that he would be joining him at the hotel. Once in front of the hotel room, Gavin knocked at the door. Derrick opened and let him in.

"Hi, Gavin, how was your night? Mine was very interesting…" Teased Derrick

"Where is Dina," asked Gavin

"I'm right here," said Dina

Gavin was surprised, the atmosphere in the room was not as tense as it was when he left, and Derrick was not as agitated as he was the day before. Much to Gavin's surprise, Derrick left him alone with Dina, pretending that he was going to take a shower. Gavin looked at Dina, she remained impassive. He realized that she was not the same person the he had dropped at this hotel room yesterday, she looked defeated and resigned. He was very concerned by the look on her face.

"How are you this morning?" Asked Gavin

"Good," replied Dina.

"Are you sure? You don't look like you're okay, Dina, what happened? Did Derrick touch you? Asked Gavin

"No, nothing happened, I simply had an unpleasant conversation with my dad last night," explained Dina

"I'm sorry to hear about that, one of my lawyers want to talk to you about the divorce." Said Gavin

"No, I won't talk to none of your lawyers, Doctor Lawrence, it's enough, I don't want to continue to live this way anymore." Replied Dina.

As soon as Gavin heard Dina calling him by his title, he knew something was really wrong.

"What do you mean Dina? I don't understand…" Said Gavin

"I mean that I'm not divorcing Derrick anymore. We have a son together, and he needs both of us." Replied Dina

"I know that your son needs both of you, Dina, that's why you are going to share his custody with Derrick." Said Gavin

"No, I don't need any custody arrangement. I'm staying with Derrick, and we will raise our son together." Stated Dina.

"Come on Dina, not again! don't do this to yourself. Listen to your heart this time." Said Gavin.

"Listen to my heart? repeated Dina cynically. I don't trust my heart anymore, Gavin. Listening to my heart is what put me in so much trouble in the first place." Replied Dina.

"I can't believe that you passed only one night in a room with Derrick and he has already brainwash you," deduced Gavin.

"It's not because of Derrick, my father was very angry at me over the phone last night. He reminded me that I'm a mother now, and that I should put my son's interest first. He even asked me to use my brain for once. That made me realize how stupid I may have been." Said Dina

"I know he is your father Dina, but I don't think he should have talked to you like that. Anyway, you don't have to do what your father wants you to do, it's your life after all, not his. I think that you are old enough to know what is best for you." Replied Gavin.

"Oh, I will listen to him this time. I have seen where not following his advice got me. I'm staying with Derrick and trying to clean up my mess." Responded Dina

"You won't be happy if you don't follow your heart, Dina." Said Gavin

"I followed my heart once and see what happened with Derrick. Now it's time for me to use a new strategy and change the direction of my life." Replied Dina.

"Please Dina, don't. Trying something new doesn't guarantee success." Said Gavin.

"Really? What happened to "you should take a chance and try something new?" or "You want to go back to your old way because you are too scared to start over?" You're the one that told me to test something different, Gavin, and you were right." Replied Dina.

"I was not talking about choosing to follow your head instead of your heart, Dina." Responded Gavin.

"Too bad, because that's definitely what I'm going to do. Here, this is your phone, thank you for letting me use it. I want you to know that I will not call you again. I also need to ask you to not contact me anymore." Said Dina.

"Unbelievable! Replied Gavin. You want to use your brain now? I hope that you use it well then, because you can follow your heart and still use your brain to make a good decision, while you cannot calculate everything with your brain and think that your heart won't suffer from it. Once you become some calculated, cold woman, there will be no place for me in your heart." Said Gavin.

"I can survive that, Gavin; my heart has been a deserted place for a while now, and I'm still standing. I have one last request, if you really love me as you pretend, I want you to promise me that if one day I become crazy enough to ask you to give you and I a try, do not listen to me. I would know that you really loved me, and hopefully, I would go back to my good sense again." Replied Dina

"Wow, I suppose it is good-bye time for us, then…" Said Gavin

"I'm afraid it is …" Replied Dina

Gavin left and closed the door behind him. Dina sat on the bed and cried her eyes out.

"You did good," said Derrick, "thank you for giving me a second chance, I promise that I will make it up to you." He added.

"Actually, that's your third chance Derrick, but who is counting, right?" Replied Dina.

"You won't be disappointed this time," promised Derrick.

Chapter 20

Dina quitted her job at the office to please Derrick, she passed her days between taking care of their son and doing housework. She also cooked every day, which was a delight for Derrick. As time passed, Dina felt bored from staying at home, so she decided to sign up for cooking classes.

The day of the first culinary lesson finally arrived. Dina went to her parents' house to drop her son. Once arrived, Dina parked her car and took Ethan from the back of the car. Then, she took his diaper bag that she had prepared and hung it over her shoulder. Finally, she locked her car and walked towards her mother who was waiting for her at the front porch of the house. Dina's mother took Ethan in her arms, and Dina handed her the baby's bag.

"I put everything he might need in this bag, mom: some diapers, wipers and another set of clothes; There are also two bottles of water and a formula dispenser. You just have to mix it when you need to feed him." Explained Dina.

"Wow is it the way that new mom like you do it now? It so easy for you guys." Joked her mother.

Dina smiled and asked:

"Is dad sleeping?"

"Yes, he had to work last night." Explained her mother

"Okay, I will see him when I come back. Bye mom, and thanks for accepting to watch Ethan for me." Said Dina before leaving.

While she was opening the driver door, Julie approached.

"Long time, no see. What are you up to lately, Dina?" Asked Julie.

"Julie! how are you? I did not see you coming." Replied Dina.

"It's been a while since you came to visit your parents, what happened?" Asked Julie.

"Nothing, I just came to drop my son before going to my cooking class." Replied Dina.

"Oh, you're taking cooking classes? Good for you! You should give me your phone number and your address, I would like to come to visit you sometimes." Said Julie.

"That's a good idea." Replied Dina.

Dina got in her car to search for a pen and a piece of paper, but Julie handed Dina her phone, and instructed her to write it on her phone instead.

"You seem in a hurry, here just write your phone number there, you will give me the address when I call you." Said Julie.

Dina wrote her phone number on Julie's cell phone and left. She was very excited while driving to her former community college. "I always loved to cook," thought Dina, "I'm sure it will be fun to learn some new recipes and make them at home."

When the cooking class ended, Dina went back to her parents' house to pick up her son. Her mother was watching news about Haiti from the internet. Dina sat down and watched with her. They were announcing that the mission of stabilization was leaving the country, and some members of the mission were accused of raping women. They were leaving illegitimate children behind, with no hope of providing any support to them.

Dina automatically thought about the women she was helping back in Haiti. She was in such a hurry to escape Derrick's investigator, that she had to close the place where they were getting helped. She felt sad, and ashamed for deserting them the way that she did. She stood up and told her mother that she was leaving.

"Bye mom, and thanks again." Said Dina

"It was a pleasure to me to pass some time with my grand-son, see you tomorrow," replied her mother.

"No, I don't have class tomorrow; it is only once a week. I will see you next week." Said Dina.

"Okay, see you next week then." Said her mother.

Gavin was gloomy and nostalgic. "I missed Dina more than I expected," he realized. "She asked me to never contact her, and I intend to respect that. I just need to know how she's doing, but I can't ask Derrick for her. Maybe I should go to visit her parents and ask them how she's doing." Thought Gavin.

The day after, Julie called Dina. They talked about their present respective lives and Dina learned that Julie and Lucas were getting married.

"I chose you as my maid of honor Dina; oh, I forget: you're married! so I should call you my "matron of honor," joked Julie. "I don't know what happened to you, but you became way too fat; you need to lose some weight before my wedding." Added Julie.

"I'm very flattered that you chose me Julie, and I promise that I will lose some weight." Said Dina

The following week, after Gavin finished to consult his patients at the office, he drove to Dina's parents', but once he arrived in the neighborhood, he drove back. "She's still a married woman, I can't just show up at her parent's house. It will be too obvious to them that I'm in love with their daughter," Thought Gavin.

Gavin was still driving in her parents' neighborhood when he spotted Dina passing by. He parked his car a few blocks away and couldn't decide if he should go to their house to see her. He was still parked there, undecided, when he saw her car leaving. He decided to follow her to try to talk to her.

As Gavin was turning the ignition key to start his car, all of the sudden, he saw someone approaching his car's window. Seeing that the person looked familiar, Gavin lowered his window.

"Are you stalking my neighbors?" Asked Julie

"Of course not, I'm a friend of their daughter," replied Gavin

"I know who you are, I was just kidding; you are Dina's boss right?" Enquired Dina.

"I was, yes, but unfortunately, she quit her job; I was going to ask her parents about her, but I changed my mind." Said Gavin.

"Why? I'm sure they will be happy to see you." Said Julie

"I don't know, it just doesn't feel right; she is someone else's wife now." Replied Gavin

"But you love her; in fact, you loved her since the night that you layed eyes on her at the night club, I could see it." Said Julie.

"I remember you, you were with her that night at the club, and the night that I picked her up at her house for the welcome party also." Realized Gavin.

"You know what, I'm getting married in a few months, and Dina is my main bridesmaid. I think you should seize this occasion to get in touch with her. I would be happy to see you there. I have a few invitation cards in my house would you mind if I ran to get you one?" Asked Julie.

"I will be happy to be there." Replied Gavin.

Months passed, and Julie's wedding day had finally arrived. Dina was overwhelmed with tasks to accomplish for Julie, but, fortunately, she got everything smooth for the wedding.

Dina was ready to go to the wedding ceremony and was waiting for Derrick who was supposed to accompany her. She called him on his cell phone, but he did not pick up. Since she did not hear from him, she decided to call Edna at the office to enquire of his whereabouts.

"Lawrence and Lee office, how can I help you?" asked a suave and charming voice on the phone.

Dina was surprised, Derrick did not tell her that they had hired a new medical assistant at the office.

"Hello…, yes," replied Dina, "I would like to talk to Dr. Lee please."

"And what is your name?" Replied the new employee.

"I'm Doctor Lee's wife, not a patient, would you be kind to put him on the phone please?" Asked Dina.

"I'm sorry but Dr. Lee is not available right now. You can leave him a message." Said firmly the employee.

Dina was about to tell her to tell Derrick that she was waiting for him to go to the wedding, but omitted to do so after she realized that he would cause her to be late if she waited on him as he was still at the office

"I will talk to him later, thank you." Replied Dina.

"You're welcome, good bye." Replied the new employee.

Dina did not know what to think, why is Derrick not picking up is cell phone, and what is he doing at the office after closing hours? She grabbed her car key, took her son, and left for the wedding.

Dina arrived just in time to help the bride.

"Gavin, what a surprise! what are you doing here?" Asked Dina

"Hi, Dina, your friend Julie invited me," replied Gavin

"Oh, I see; I wonder why she never told me that you were coming." Said Dina

"Hello, Doctor Lawrence!" Said Julie, "thank you for coming."

"Thank you for inviting me, you look amazing." Replied Gavin

"Thank you!" said Julie.

"And he's a gentleman," murmured Julie to Dina

"Dina is looking for someone to watch her purse, so she can help me with my dress, would you please do me the favor to hold it for her?" Asked Julie.

"It's ok," replied Dina, "I will manage," she added.

"It will be my pleasure," replied Gavin.

Dina handed her purse to Gavin and escorted him to an empty chair near a window. Gavin profited to chat with Dina.

"So, how are you?" Asked Gavin.

"I'm okay, what about you?" Replied Dina.

"I'm holding on…" Said Gavin.

Gavin was waiting for Dina to ask him what he was holding on to, but she did not ask. On the contrary, she put an end at their conversation and went to help Julie. "Wow, Dina really wants to make her marriage work with Derrick, she's avoiding me at all costs," Thought Gavin.

Julie's wedding festivity was finally over, Dina was very tired. When Julie asked her to be her matron of honor, she thought it was going to be a simple rehearsal, and the wedding ceremony, following by a reception. Dina, who used to participate in Haitian's wedding only, did not expect that there will be a bridal party, and a bachelorette party in top of that. In just a few months, she was able to put all the bridesmaids' suggestions together and presented them to Julie and Lucas. After consensus, they went ahead, and planned every single detail of the wedding.

After the wedding, Julie called Dina to express her gratitude.

"I just wanted to thank you. All my friends and family are telling me how well organized the wedding was." Said Julie.

"Thanks, it was my pleasure to be your matron of honor," said Dina

"By the way," said Julie, "did you know that your former boss, Doctor Lawrence, is getting married next month? Asked Julie

"No, I was not aware. How did you now?" Asked Dina.

"He just sent me an invitation," Said Julie.

"So, are you going?" Asked Dina.

"No, I don't think it would be fair to go to the wedding of the man that my matron of honor is in love with, when she's not the one that will have the joy to marry him." Said Julie.

"I'm already married, Julie," Replied Dina.

"I know, but you're not happy in your marriage, and do you know why? Because you are in love with Doctor Lawrence." Presumed Julie.

"I know that I shouldn't tell you that because you just got married, but who said that people must be happy in their marriage? Anyway, Gavin is in love with someone else, and I'm happy for him." Said Dina

"How do you know he's in love?" Asked Julie.

"Well, he's getting married, there must be something between them," argued Dina.

"All I know is that the man that I found parked in our parent's neighborhood, spying, just to have a glimpse of you, is in love with *you*. If I were you, I would go and try to talk him over marrying someone else. In case that he listens to you and call off the wedding, you should get a divorce and marry him." Explained Julie.

"That's not going to happen," answered Dina.

But at Dina's surprise, she was dressed and was standing at the entrance of the church, the day of the rehearsal. Many people started to arrive but there was no trace of Gavin yet.

"What am I doing here" Thought Dina, "that's not fair to just show up in someone's rehearsal with the objective of seducing the groom to be."

Dina stood out of the church and walked away to get to her car. While she was putting the key inside the door to open it, a car pulled up near hers. Dina heard someone coming towards her. She instinctively turned, and saw it was Gavin, dressed in blue jeans, and a purple shirt.

"Dina, how are you? But what are you doing here? Asked Gavin.

"I'm fine thank you. I learned that you're getting married and I have not received any invitation yet." Said Dina.

"I'm sure that you did not come for an invitation, Dina, since I know that you wouldn't want to take any part in my wedding. Why don't you just tell me to what I owe the honor of your presence at my wedding rehearsal?" Asked Gavin.

"You are wrong to think that I don't want to participate in your wedding, Gavin. You have been there for me on most of my haziest days and have rejoiced with me on my fluky ones. It's going to be one of the happiest days of your life, and I would like to witness it, and for once, be there for you too." Replied Dina.

"Are you trying to stop my wedding, Dina?" Asked Gavin.

"Of course not. You know I'm not that kind of person." Lied Dina.

"Well, when you suddenly discover that you're in love with someone, you can do things that you don't usually do. I should know." Replied Gavin.

"Let us suppose that I came here to try to stop your wedding, would you consider giving *us* a chance, you and I?" Asked Dina.

"*Us*? There is no us, Dina! You married Derrick, even though I pleaded to you to do not do so. You also made me promise that, if one day you are crazy enough to ask me to give *us* a try, to do not listen to you, if I really love you. Guess what? I really love you! That's the only promise you had requested from me, I intend to keep that promise." Replied Gavin.

Dina got in her car and left. She could not believe that she had let go the love of her life because she was too stubborn to listen to her heart, and to Gavin also.

The day of Gavin's wedding, Dina was feeling very depressed. She felt the urge to go to dance and drink, so she decided to go the Antillean nightclub. Dina called the babysitter to stay with her son and drove to the club.

Chapter 21

When Dina arrived at the club, she ordered a beer, and sat on a corner. A gentleman came to her table, presented himself and sat with her. He asked if he could buy her a drink, but she refused. Seeing that Dina was barely talking to him, the gentleman asked her to dance, but Dina declined, pretending that she was tired, and was there just for the ambience. The gentleman left without further persistence.

Dina was looking at the couples dancing on the stage, the same stage where she and Gavin had once danced. But tonight, Gavin was getting married, and he will never dance with her anymore.

She was still thinking about Gavin, when something caught her attention: someone who looked exactly like Gavin was standing in front of her. "I think I had too much drink, the alcohol is impairing my sense of reality." Thought Dina. She closed her eyes, shook slightly her head, and reopened her eyes. She saw that Gavin was still standing in front of her. "I know you're just in my head, but you look so real," she said mostly to herself.

"Well, that's because I am real," Gavin replied.

"Gavin! what are you doing here? aren't you supposed to be at your wedding right now?" Asked Dina.

"There was no wedding. I could not go through with it," Replied Gavin.

"Really!?" Said Dina, surprised and happy.

"Yeah," confirmed Gavin.

"How did you know I was here?" Asked Dina.

"Because I was once in your shoes. The day you were marrying Derrick, I came here Dina, the place where we first met. I thought there was a good chance that you would come here today too." Said Gavin.

"What about the bride, is she going to be okay?" asked Dina.

"I think so, I don't mean to be rude, but I think she was more interested to marry my title than me." Replied Gavin.

"Well, I like the title also," teased Dina.

"Is that so," replied Gavin, amused.

"So, what now?" Asked Dina

"Now is time for love, Dina, will you marry me?" Asked Gavin while opening a box.

Dina saw a ring in the box and could not hold her laugh.

"You're supposed to give me an answer, Dina, not laughing at me," said happily Gavin.

"Oh no, no, I was not laughing at you. I was thinking about our situation. I'm still a married woman, and another man is asking me to marry him on his wedding day; sounds crazy, doesn't it? Asked Dina

"Why does it have to be so complicated with you, Dina! You came to my wedding rehearsal to persuade me to give our love a try, and that's what I'm trying to do right now. Do you want me to wait for tomorrow to propose to you? Replied Gavin.

"No. Actually, I would prefer that you go back to your fiancée and marry her. Sitting here alone allowed me to reflect on our relationship, and I realized that I need to save my marriage. What if you were right? Said Dina.

"Right about what, Dina?" asked Gavin. "I don't have any idea of what you're talking about," he added.

"I'm always running away. In fact, I'm incapable of facing up my problems, the only strategy that I have is to run for the hills. I don't want to continue to live like that, and more importantly, I don't want to put you through this a second time." Said Dina.

"Come on Dina, not again! don't do this to me, to us. I just abandoned a woman at the altar to pursue you because I'm in love with you. So, if you're in love with me too, let's just started a new life together. No more games, it's now or never." Said Gavin.

"You don't understand, I have enough of running away every time that I'm facing difficulties. This time, I want to stay and fight. I want to fight for my marriage which is in jeopardy, I owe it to my son. I'm going home to talk to Derrick to see how we can work together to save our marriage." Replied Dina.

"What about us, Dina?" Asked Gavin

"There's no us, as you once said. I'm a married woman, go back to your fiancée, maybe she will forgive you, and give you a second chance." Replied Dina

"I came here solely to ask you to divorce Derrick and marry me. If you let me get out of this place without any hope that our love will prevail, don't even think about contacting me once you change your mind. You said that you are tired of running every time that you are facing a challenging situation but that is exactly what you are doing right now, you are running away from our love." Said Gavin.

"No, I just feel the need to work on my marriage instead of giving up." Argued Dina

"So why do you look so sad? And why did you come here, the place that we first met, on my wedding day?" Asked Gavin.

"Because we were close, and I'm just scared that once you're married, you would forget about me." Explained Dina

"Well, you still chose Derrick, you can't have it both ways. I need stability in my life and this situation is far from being a stable one. Let me simplify it for you: from now on, I'm going to cut all contacts between us, so you can really focus on having a happy marriage with Derrick." Replied Gavin.d

"I'm really sorry that I deceive you, it was not my intention to hurt you in any way," said sadly Dina.

"Don't feel sorry for me, I will be alright. Just focus on making things work with Derrick, if it's more important to you." Replied Gavin.

Gavin put his hands in his pockets and walked away. Dina ordered drinks after drinks, until the bartender refused to serve her more alcoholic drinks, claiming that he can be sued for over-serving her alcohol. After paying, Dina stood up to leave but stumbled back on the chair. She felt someone lifting her, putting her in the back of a car, and driving away with her.

When the car finally stopped, the same person got out the car, picked her up, and walked with her to her house. Dina was so wasted that she didn't recognized who was holding her into those strong arms. Once in front of the house, the person rang the entrance door, and Dina saw the babysitter opening the door. Dina let herself in and collapsed on the nearest sofa.

When Dina woke up, she went to her room and saw that Derrick was sleeping in the bed. She went to the bathroom, brushed her teeth and took a shower. Then, she went to her son's room, and kissed him good night.

When Dina went back to her room to sleep, she found Derrick sitting on the bed, waiting for her.

"Where were you?" asked an angry Derrick.

"What?" asked Dina, surprised.

"I'm asking you where you went today, Dina" repeated Derrick.

Oh, no, why did he want to know where I was? Does he know that I was depressed about Gavin getting married, what should I said to deflate this situation? Asked Dina to herself.

"I went for a drink, and had the time to think about us, I have decided to work harder to save our marriage." Explained Dina.

"That's so ironic! You went to have a drink with a man that had just abandoned his fiancée at the altar, to finally take the resolution to save our marriage?" Replied Derrick.

"Believe it or not, that's the truth," said Dina

"The truth is, Gavin will never leave you alone, and you will always love him." Replied Derrick.

"I don't know what you're talking about." Said Dina.

"Then let me tell you what I'm talking about, Dina, I'm talking about the man that dropped my drunk wife on my porch tonight, you are aware that we have a camera at the front door, don't you?" Asked Derrick.

Dina was surprised, she realized that was Gavin that lifted her in his arms and drove her home.

"It's not what it looks like, we have said goodbye to each other tonight, you have nothing to worry about from now one." Replied Dina.

"He will never leave you alone!" Yelled Derrick.

"He will, I personally asked him to, and Gavin always tries to keep his promise." Said Dina

"Well, Gavin just *trying* to stay away from you is not enough for me! I want him to leave you alone for good, and for this to happen, I need to talk to him."

Dina and Derrick went to counselling to help them resolve their issues and save their marriage. She focused on being the wife that Derrick wanted. She became a housewife who had the responsibility to take care of her husband and their son.

Derrick was often absent. For some time now, he started going to work early, and coming home late at night.

"What am I doing wrong? Why is my husband avoiding me like that? It's like he's living at the office now. I clean, cook, wash and iron his clothes, and it's still not enough to bring him home right after work. I think I might have to try something new to get us closer again." Thought Dina.

Dina knew that Derrick loved football, so, she went online, and brought two tickets for the next game.

When the day of the game had arrived, Dina called her mother to stay with her son. When her mother arrived, Dina took a shower, dressed up, and left.

"I am just going to drop by his office to take him to the game." Though Dina. As she was parking her car, she saw that there was another car that she did not recognize, parked beside Derrick's car. "Maybe it's Gavin's new car," thought Dina. It was not unusual for Gavin to buy a new car from time to time.

Dina locked her door and proceeded to enter the office buildings. It was already 6:00 pm, and the football game was starting at 6:30 pm. Once in the building, Dina realized that the office door was closed. She knocked on the door, but no one answered.

"That's weird," thought Dina, "why is Gavin's car parked here, and he's not opening the door. Let me just call him, then."

Dina opened her purse, took her phone, and called Derrick.

"Hello, Dina? Is everything alright?" Asked Derrick.

"Yes," answered Dina, "It's just that I..." Started Dina, but Derrick abruptly interrupted her:

"Listen...I'm still at the office, and I'm very busy. I have a few things to check before I leave." Said Derrick.

"Well, can't you let someone else take care of it for you?" Asked Dina.

"No, everyone else had already left, I'm alone at the office, I have to check everything myself. So, see you in a few hours." Replied Derrick.

Dina didn't know what to think, there was another car parked near Derrick's, how could he tell her that he was alone? "it just doesn't make sense," thought Dina.

Dina went back to her car and drove away. But she realized that Derrick sounded like he was not himself on the phone.

"What if he's in danger?" She thought, "what if someone is holding him against his will?" She thought about calling the police but restrain to do so when she imagined what a fool she would look like if she was wrong.

Dina decided to park her car nearby and watch what was going on. She held on her phone to dial the emergency number just in case that her suspicions were right. She was looking carefully at the building entrance. After about twenty minutes, she saw Derrick coming out, arm on arm with a woman.

"Oh no, not again Derrick... Please, not again..." Murmured Dina to herself.

Dina didn't move. This time, she didn't want to confront Derrick. "What am I going to do?" thought Dina, "if I try to leave him, he might take Ethan away. Think Dina! Think fast! Okay, as dad had reminded me, I have a brain, and I need to use it right now!"

Suddenly, Dina had an idea: "What if I record them?"

Dina put her phone on low light, pressed the recording button, and started filming Derrick and the woman. Derrick went to open the driver door for the woman, she entered the car, and Derrick stood up near her door. They seemed to be in an animated conversation, then, Derrick approached his face near the woman's face, and they kissed...

Dina uttered a groan, she could not believe that Derrick was cheating on her once more after he promised to never do it again.

Derrick thought that he heard a muffled groan coming from the alley...

"It's getting late, we shouldn't stay here. Let's go somewhere else, I will follow you." Said Derrick to the woman.

Dina immediately stopped recording and hid behind the wheel. After they both left, she went straight to her house. Dina told her mother everything and showed her the video that she had recorded.

"That explains why he's never around. I was always against divorce, but now, I understand why some people have to take that road. You can't stay with that man, he's getting worse and worse every day. What are you going to do now?" Asked her mother.

"Mom, I want you to keep my phone, that's the only proof of Derrick's infidelity that I have. I'm going to wait for him and tell him that I'm leaving with Ethan. If he threatens to take sole custody of Ethan, I will tell him about the video." Replied Dina

"Alright, be careful, okay," Said her mother.

"Okay, bye mom". Replied Dina.

Chapter 22

Around 10:00 p.m., Dina heard one of the garage doors opening. She knew that Derrick was here. She sat down on the bed and waited for him.

"Hi, how are you? Sorry I couldn't come right away, I was very busy." Said Derrick.

"Yeah, it seemed like you were in the middle of something…" Replied Dina.

"Yes, it was a busy day… I'm really tired, let me take a shower and I will rejoin you in the bed." Said Derrick.

Dina was thinking, "is it for real? I can't believe this man! He came here acting like nothing had happened. It must not be the first time that he had been with her."

"You have to be kidding me!" replied Dina.

"I'm sorry?" Asked Derrick.

"No, you are not sorry Derrick, you are just a pathetic cheater! You were with that woman this afternoon, and tonight you came home acting like nothing had happened. I'm sure that's where you are every night, but today you just got caught!" Said Dina.

"What are you talking about, Dina?" Asked Derrick.

"I'm talking about the kiss that you two had exchanged and that I recorded on my phone." Explained boldly Dina.

Derrick's face passed from pale to livid. He walked towards Dina, and shouted "Give me your phone, now!"

"Stop yelling at me, I don't have it," said Dina.

"Give me that video, or I will throw you out and take sole custody of Ethan. You know what I'm capable of doing to you, right?" Replied Gavin.

"Right, but with that video, I think that you are the one that should worry about what I can do to you, Derrick. The video had a good image of you and that woman, you're sure that you want to see it on every social media?" Said Dina.

"You wouldn't." replied Derrick.

"You're right I wouldn't because all I want, is to be part of my son's life. You can keep the house and everything else, I don't want anything from you, Derrick." Said Dina.

Derrick was surprised. He didn't think that Dina would voluntary leave everything to him, and was ready to move on, and that rankled him.

"Where will you be staying?" Asked Derrick

"Don't worry about me, I will find a place to stay," Replied Dina

"Of course, you will, you are planning on moving in with Gavin!" Shouted Derrick

"I am not planning anything with Gavin yet, Derrick, it's about *you* now, not me. Once again, you have cheated on me, and I'm just making sure that this time, you've betrayed me for the last time.

"I promise that's the last time," said Derrick with a soft voice

"No, enough Derrick, I am leaving you, and I am taking Ethan with me." Replied Dina

"I can't let you do that, Dina." Said Derrick

"There is nothing you can do about it." Replied Dina

"You can leave if you want, but If you take Ethan, I will get your black ass arrested for kidnapping." Said Derrick

"You are so pathetic, every time that you are mad at me, you are threatening my blackness. I am going to fight tooth and nail for Ethan, Derrick. I am not taking him with me tonight, but I will be back to get him." Replied Dina

Dina stood up, took a luggage and dropped a few clothes in it. When she arrived at the front door, she turned and said:

"See you in court, Derrick."

"If you do that you will lose, Dina, and I will make sure that you are prohibited to see Ethan." Replied Derrick.

"I would be worried about my video going viral on social media if I were you, Derrick. The woman that you were with surely has a boyfriend or a husband, but you were the one fondling and kissing with her last night." Said Dina, who took her luggage and left.

Four months had passed, and Dina was still living with her parents. She tried to find a job, so she could hire a lawyer who would force

Derrick to let her see her son, but she just couldn't find any. Dina realized that most of the medical assistant job posting now stipule that any candidate for the post should be able to speak Spanish. Ted was working two jobs to take care of his twins, but he could not see them.

One afternoon, Julie and her husband Lucas came to visit Julie's parent, and they learn that Dina was livingving with her parents now. Julie and her husband profited to come by Dina's house and chatted with her.

"How is your son," asked Julie. "Mom and dad said they hadn't seen him around, where is he?"

Dina explained to Julie what had happened. Julie asked to watch the video, which Dina played it for her.

"You have this video on him, and you let him bar you from seeing your son? Wow!" Said Julie

"He knows that I was bluffing, that I will never share his video online,"

"Why not?" Asked Julie, "he absolutely deserves it." Argued Julie

"He's the father of my son; this video could embarrass him." Explained Dina

"You cared too much about someone who doesn't give a damn about you. What about Doctor Lawrence, what does he think about all of this?" Asked Julie.

"I don't know I haven't contacted him." Replied Dina.

"I would be surprised if he never tried to get in touch with you." Said Julie.

"I asked him to never contact me." Replied Dina.

"Why would you ask him to do that?" Enquired Julie

"Because I'm in love with him, and I knew that with him in the picture, my relationship with Derrick would be in jeopardy. I just wanted to save my marriage with Derrick, I am such an idiot" Avowed Dina

"Well, why don't you try to contact Doctor Lawrence now, he is so into you, I am sure that he will forgive you, and will even help you to get custody of your son." Said Julie

"No way, I just need to find a job and retain the service of a lawyer," replied Dina

"Okay, you do that, you must be missing your son a lot." Said Julie

"You have no idea," said Dina, while fighting back tears.

After Julie and her husband left, Dina went to her room, locked her door and let her tears flow. Then, she opened her computer and went to Gavin's social page. Nothing has change for him, "he either has no girlfriend presently or he did not include her in his page," thought Dina.

Once at home, Julie search for Gavin's number, and called him

When Gavin learned about Dina's situation, he immediately called her and set up an appointment with her to see a lawyer.

A few weeks later, the landline phone of Dina's parent rang, and it was Derrick, he wanted to know if Dina could come to watch

The day of the custody hearing arrived, Dina was surprised to see Gavin at the court.

"Everything is going to be alright okay. Edmund told me that he's certain the judge will approve your request to have your son leaving with you. Derrick will have him on week-ends only." Said Gavin.

As predicted, Dina won primary custody of her son. Gavin invited Dina and her parents to join him at a restaurant, to celebrate the victory.

"You guys go ahead, we have to go home to prepare a room for Ethan." Said Dina's parents

The restaurant was a little bit too crowded for Dina.

"Today is Friday," explained Gavin, "everybody comes here because that's one of the rare chic restaurants where you can drop by to eat without a reservation. But I will make it up to you, I'm going to make a reservation in a more discreet restaurant, and I will surprise you." Promised Gavin.

"You don't have to." Said Dina

"I know, but I just want to…it's been a long time, I'm glad to see you." Replied Gavin

"Me too," admitted Dina

"By the way, you look…great." Said Gavin

"Thank you." Replied Dina

"Why didn't you call me to let me know what was happening?" Asked Gavin

"Well, I didn't hear from you for a while, I was not sure if I should contact you or not." Replied Dina

"You asked me to never contact you, Dina." Said Gavin

"Yes but, not for so long, you didn't even come when Derrick organized that birthday party for me." Replied Dina

"I was not invited; don't tell me you didn't know?" Said Dina

"Sorry, I didn't know," replied Dina

After they finished to eat, Gavin dropped Dina at her parent's house, and left.

"Today was a good day," thought Dina, "it's been a while since I had such a good time."

"Mommy, can I play outside?" Asked Ethan.

It's been three weeks since he had been living with Dina and her parents, and he love to play on the front yard.

"No, not now baby, wait for mommy to finish to cook, she will go to play with you, Ok?" Said Dina

"Okay, Mommy" Replied Ethan

The entrance door rang, Dina went to see, it was Gavin

Dina opened, Gavin had flowers in one hand, and a wrapped gift in the other. He handed the flower to Dina and asked her if he could give the present to Ethan.

"You got flowers mommy," Said Ethan

"Yes," said Dina, "and guess who else get something?" she added

"Granma?" Asked Ethan

"No, you," said Gavin

"Who is he, mommy?" Asked Ethan

"It's Gavin, baby; mommy's friend." Replied Dina.

"And guess what?" Said Gavin "I brought this just for you. You want to open it?"

Ethan looked at his mother who gave him the signal to accept it. He took it and was about to open it

"Didn't you forget to say something to Gavin," asked his mother.

"Thank you," said Ethan

Ethan hastily opened his present. "it's a foot-all," he shouted

"Football," corrected Dina, amused. "Repeat after me: football."

'Foot-ball," repeated Ethan.

"Good job," encouraged Dina.

"Can I play with it?" asked Ethan

"Yes, but not inside the house, why don't you wait a few minutes? I'm almost done with the cooking." Replied Dina

"Can Davin play with me?" Asked Ethan.

"His name is *Gavin*, okay; say it like that: *Gavin*," said Dina

"Gavin," repeated Ethan.

Say it again, said Dina.

"*Gavin*, *Gavin*, *Gavin*" repeated Ethan.

"Good job," said Dina, "you got it."

"Can I play with Gavin, now?" Asked Ethan

"No, I don't think that Gavin has the time to..." started Dina

"Sure, I have plenty of time. Do you want me to play with him outside?" Asked Gavin

"Yes, please, he's been asking me to go outside with him for a while now." Said Dina.

Gavin and Ethan were playing football on the front yard. Dina finally finished to cook and went to them. She stood there for a moment and watched them play together. They seemed to be getting along great. Gavin was so kind and patient with Ethan, Dina did not know that side of him, and it made her feelings for him stronger.

"Mommy," said Ethan, "do you want to play with us?"

"No, I came to tell you guys that dinner is ready," said Dina. And, addressing to Gavin she Asked "I made rice with chicken in sauce, would you like to join us."

"Sure, after you," he said while holding the door to let Dina and Ethan inside.

Gavin and Ethan went to wash their hands, then, they sat at the table, prayed, and ate. After they finished to eat, Dina picked up the empty plates from the table. Gavin stood up and helped her to place the dirty plates on the sink. He profited to thank Dina for the food and told her that he tried to call her before coming to let her know that he was dropping by, but that her phone was not working.

"Yeah, we are experiencing a problem with the phone, but you don't have to phone before you come, you can just drop by" said Dina. "I'm mostly at home applying for medical assistant jobs on the internet."

"Why don't you go back to law school?" Asked Gavin.

"Nah, it's a lot, I don't think I will be able to focus on my studies anymore." Replied Dina.

"Why?" Asked Gavin

"Well, with everything that is going on in my life right now, I don't think it's the right things to do. I'm more focus on finding a job." Said Dina

"With a degree in law, you will make more money you know." Replied Gavin.

"I like being a medical assistant," said Dina

"I understand, but you might be better as a lawyer," insisted Gavin.

"Are you assuming that I was not a good medical assistant?" Asked Dina with a smile

"You are a good medical assistant, but you can be a great lawyer, Dina," said Gavin.

"Well, I will think about it." Said Dina

"I must leave now, thank you for the dinner, bye, bye Ethan." Said Gavin.

One week later, Gavin came to pick up Dina. She left her son with her parents.

"Where are we going?" asked Dina.

"It's a surprise." Said Gavin.

When Gavin arrived at the place, a valet attendant took his keys to park the car, and him and Dina entered inside the restaurant where Gavin gave his full name. Dina realized that he had reserved their table.

A hostess came and presented them the menus. Dina looked at the costs of the dishes and saw how high the prices were.

"This is a very expensive restaurant, and it's not easy to get a reservation. You didn't have to do all of this." Said Dina.

"It was not that difficult to reserve here, anyway, I promised it to you." Replied Gavin.

They had a good time together at the restaurant, laughing and talking about Ethan, the way he says things, and how curious he is. Then, Gavin went to pick up his car to drop Dina at her parent's house.

While he was driving, Gavin told Dina that he heard Derrick was getting remarried. Dina was so surprised that she was quiet for the rest of the ride. When Gavin arrived in front of her house, he kissed her on the cheek, and left. Dina did not say a word, she went straight to her room and wept. How did Derrick dare to move on so fast? Remarried? Why is it so easy for him to just wipe away everything they shared and replace her that fast?

Chapter 23

Gavin was driving in circles, he did not know what to think. He thought that Dina was in love with him, but then she became very sad when she learned that Derrick was about to get married again.

"I need to talk to her, I need her to tell me exactly why she is upset about that." Thought Gavin.

The day after, Gavin went back to talk to Dina. When he rang at the door, Dina's father opened. He was going to work, so, he gave Gavin a seat, and called Dina's mother to keep him company in the living room, while Dina was getting ready to see him.

When Dina finally came, her mother left, to go to make some coffee.

"You're up early," said Dina, when she finally came to him.

"Yes, I couldn't sleep last night, and I can tell that you didn't sleep a wink also by your face appearance, you look tired Dina," said Gavin.

"Well, I was surprised when you told me that Derrick was already getting remarried," replied Dina.

"I figured that out," said Gavin

"I'm glad you came, I wanted to talk to you too," replied Dina.

"Really?" Asked Gavin.

"Yes, I wanted to thank you for everything you have done for me and Ethan. Last night you and I had a good night at the restaurant, eating and enjoying each other." Said Dina

"We did," agreed Gavin

"I wanted to tell you that... I know I messed up by not accepting to marry you the first time that you asked me to, and..., if you are still in love with me, and that the marriage proposition is still standing, it would be my honor to marry you." Said Dina.

"I can't believe you Dina! When are you going to think before taking any big decisions in your life?" Asked Gavin.

"What do you mean? Of course, I thought about it! I passed the night thinking about us. I thought you were thinking about me also, and that we were at the same page. Apparently, I was wrong, you don't love me anymore." Said Dina.

"Of course, I still love you, but I don't want you to accept to marry me just because your ex-husband is getting married. If we are going to have a real future together, it must be based on our feelings for one another, not on someone else's situation." Replied Gavin.

"So, you didn't come here to ask me to marry you? Why did you come to see me this early then?" asked Dina.

"I wanted to know why you were so sad last night, when you learned about Derrick's upcoming wedding." Replied Gavin.

"Well, I guess that's because he is the father of my son." Explained Dina.

"Or maybe, you are still attracted to him." Argued Gavin.

"You know that you are the one that I'm attracted to, why are you doubting it." Said Dina.

"So why did you want us to get married as soon as you hear the news about Derrick? It sounds like you finally accepted to marry me just because Derrick is going to get married again. As much as I want to marry you, Dina, I think it is the wrong reason for us to get married." Said Gavin.

"And what would be a good reason for us to get married, Gavin? At least this time you can't accuse me of getting married for revenge!" Exploded Dina.

"What about love, Dina, have you ever thought about it? People should get married solely because they are in love, it is that simple. But of course, it's the least of your worries, right?" Alleged Gavin.

"Why would you think that I don't care about love? I love you, and I know that you love me. You even asked me to marry you some time ago. That's the reason why I thought we should go ahead and get married." Said Dina.

"If you really think that, getting married at the same time as Derrick does not basically sets a base for an unhealthy marriage, you are not ready to marry me, Dina." Replied Gavin.

"Why does it matter? After his wedding you will argue that it is too soon to get married, right? So, tell me, *Derrick*, when will it be the right time for you and I to get married? Asked Dina.

Dina was in shock, she could not believe what came out of her mouth, that she had called Gavin "*Derrick.*" "What if Gavin was right, what if I were in fact still attracted to Derrick?" She thought.

"I'm not *Derrick*, Dina, I'm Gavin. And the right time for you and me to get married should be when you would want to be my wife, instead of planning to start a wedding competition with Derrick to get his attention." Replied Gavin.

Gavin stood up right away, walked to the entrance door, and without turning, told Dina to say goodbye to her mother on his behalf. Then, he opened the door, closed it behind him, and left. Dina heard his car leaving, and for the first time in her life, she did not want to run and hide, nor did she cry. It was like, by closing that door, Gavin was opening the reality door for her. "you messed up big this time, but now, you have to stay to pick up the pieces of the broken glass, so that you or anyone else can't be hurt by them. All is for the best," Said Dina to herself.

Dina went to her mother in the kitchen, and without saying a word, she took a cup, poured some Haitian coffee that her mother had made, and drink it as is.

"Well, that's a first, you did not add any sugar," asked her mother.

"Yes, I wanted to taste it like that," explained Dina.

"So, do you like it?" Questioned her mother.

"Yes, it's bitter, and unsweet, and strong…" Said Dina

"Wow, you are becoming a strong woman, welcome to the club." Said her mother.

"Thanks, but how can you tell?" Asked Dina.

"The fragile girl that I knew, would be in her room right now, crying. But instead, here you are drinking unsweet coffee; that's how I know" Explained her mother

"I am a mess mom," said Dina

"You were a mess, but now I'm glad that you are on the path of turning your life around." Replied her mother.

"I love you mom," Said Dina.

"I love you too," replied her mother.

Dina left her mother in the kitchen and went in Ethan's room. She stood up for a while, looking at him. Ethan was sleeping like Derrick used to. His knees were pushed into his upper body and his elbows were joined.

"Wow," thought Dina, "Ethan took a lot from his father." She then closed the door half way and went to her room.

Once in her room, Dina took a pen and a notebook, and started writing random notes about the way she wanted to live:

Find a job; moving in her own apartment with Ethan; go to vacation with him. Before she even realized it, she had written a lot of notes, and it was in clustering type. She went ahead and started reading her notes. She realized that she was not making any progress in her life, as finding a job, and moving in her own apartment were still her primary goals after she obtained her medical assistant diploma.

"I need to do better than that," thought Dina, "I need to get a better career. Maybe I should continue my law studies online, but I still need to find a job to pay for my tuition."

After brainstorming all her goals on the paper, Dina took the notebook, bent her knees, and prayed to God on it. Then, she brushed her teeth, took a shower, and went to help her mother.

"You did not ask me what happened with Gavin, mom," said Dina.

"I was not sure if you were ready to talk about it," replied her mother

"I think I am, it is a painful period of my life, but I am about to start a new pleasant chapter," said Dina

"I'm glad that you have such a great attitude in the face of all this," replied her mother.

"Well, I used to be discouraged, to run and hide, to not feel the pain. None of these had ever helped me resolve any matter. Derrick is getting remarried, and Gavin just told me that I wanted to marry him right away because I wanted to get Derrick's attention. Although it was rude, I realized that it was also true. Every time I get rid of Derrick, I always find a way to let him back in my life. I know that we have a son together but sharing his custody should be our only link. I know that I don't love him anymore, but for some reason, knowing that he was getting married again bothered me, and I think that Gavin saw it, and took it to that extent because he thinks that I still love Derrick. And to make matters worse, I accidentally called him Derrick." Said Dina.

"I understand why he's skeptical about your true feelings for him, because when you had the choice, you chose Derrick. But about accidentally calling him Derrick, this is the kind of things that happened when you were accustomed to someone, it has nothing to do with love," replied her mother.

"Well, now he has made his choice to do not believe me, and I accepted it. I refuse to be consumed by all of this, I know I have a lot on my plate, but if God wants, I will be victorious." Said Dina

The entrance door opened, it was Ted with his twins. Him and Angel had reconciled, and they were living together, again. Ted told his family that he did the sacrifice to live with Angel, so that his kids could have both of their parents under one roof to take care of them. But Dina's family believed that Ted and Angel could not stay away from each other for long, and that was the real reason for their reconciliation.

Days went by, then weeks, and then months; and Dina hadn't heard from Gavin. She realized that she deeply missed him. She used to miss Derrick, but it wasn't the gut-wrenching solitude she felt when Gavin left. She found a part-time job as a medical assistant in a nearby hospital. She also started taking online classes at the Global University where they accepted most of the credits that she earned at the community college which will allow her to obtain a bachelor's degree in two years. Then she could enroll in their J.D. program for another two years to become a lawyer.

Chapter 24

Dina was taking care of Ethan before preparing herself. It was her graduation day, and Ethan needed to be very presentable. As Ted and Angela moved from Maryland to Pennsylvania with their twin boys, they could not attend Dina's graduation. Dina received five graduation tickets to distribute to her family members and friends, but she only had Ethan and her parents to invite.

"Go to prepare yourself, mommy, I can take care of myself, I'm 7 now." Said Ethan.

He was as excited as Dina. The graduation was being held at the university campus, and Dina did not want to be late. As soon as they arrived, Dina went to the side of the campus where the graduates were supposed to form lines before walking to the stadium, were the guests, faculty members and staff were waiting. After each student had received their diploma, they asked the graduates to turn their tassels to the left.

The graduation ceremony was finished, and the graduates were reunited with their family to take pictures.

"Daddy!" said Ethan; "mommy look, daddy is here, daddy came to your graduation!"

Dina was surprised, she wanted to tell Derrick that he had no right to be at her graduation, after the way he treated her. But she did not make any comments because she did not want Ethan to witness any arguments between them.

"Hi, Dina. Mr. and Mrs. Joseph, How are you?" Asked Derrick. "Congratulations Dina, you made it! I brought these flowers for you," said Derrick while handing them to Dina.

"Thank you," said Dina. She took them and passed them right away to her mother.

"Would you please hold them for me, mom?" Asked Dina.

"Sure," answered her mother, while taking the flowers.

"Can we both take a picture with Ethan?" Asked Derrick.

"Okay," agreed Dina. She was determined to not let Derrick get under her skin.

After taking pictures, Derrick proposed to Dina to take Ethan and her, as well as her parents to a restaurant to celebrate.

"No, thank you," said Dina. "My mother had already prepared a family meal, so we can celebrate together at home."

"Well, I guess I better get going." Said Derrick.

"Can Daddy come home with us too?" Asked Ethan.

"No, baby, daddy is busy; maybe for your graduation we can all be together to celebrate, okay?" replied Dina.

"I'm not busy at all. It would be my pleasure to participate at the celebration of your achievements." Said Derrick.

"Please mommy, say yes, say yes." Begged Ethan.

"Derrick, can I speak to you for a minute?" Asked Dina

"Sure," replied Derrick.

"This way," indicated Dina.

Dina pulled Derrick over to the closest area where it was the least crowded.

"You look stunning today. I've missed you so much., I miss what we once had." Said Derrick.

"Listen, Derrick," said abruptly Dina, "I really appreciate that you took the time to come to my graduation, but it would not be fair for your wife if I let you in my house."

"I'm divorced, Dina," replied Derrick. "I have been divorced for the past two years," explained Derrick, who was constantly looking around.

"Well, I'm sorry to learn that, but I'm still not letting you in my house, I don't want to send mix messages to our son. I think that his wellbeing should be our biggest priority." Said Dina

"I completely agree with you and that is why I came today to make amends." Said Derrick.

Right away, he pulled out a little box from his pocket, opened it, and presented it to Dina, and asked: "Dina, will you marry me again?"

Dina was furious, why would Derrick think that she would be interested in remarrying him? Without realizing it, she started uttering:

"You've broken my heart once

Then I came back so strong

That now you're the one that needs me

But I don't think we're meant to be"

"What are you saying?" Asked Derrick.

"What I'm saying, Derrick, is that I will never remarry you, I'm not in love with you. Even the first time, I should have never marry you. From now on, anything between you and I should be about Ethan, not us. I know that you love playing games, but I will not let you gamble with our son's emotions." Said Dina.

"Come on Dina, you saw it, Ethan is the one that wanted me to join at your celebration in the first place. I think there is something else; it's Gavin, right? Are you still seeing him?" Asked Derrick

"No, not that I don't want to, but Gavin decided that's the way it should be. I didn't have any say in it. It's funny though, I encountered him when my heart was still recovering from your betrayal; he was there, yet, all I wanted to see, was you. But today, when I saw you, I wished that it was him instead that come to my graduation. I'm in love with Gavin, Derrick, but you were right, he's not the type of man that would ever marry me." Said Dina

"Well, let's just prove him wrong! Dina Joseph, will you marry me?" Asked Gavin

Dina was in disbelief, she didn't see Gavin coming, she didn't even know for how long he had been there, listening to her conversation with Derrick. She was not sure if she should say yes to Gavin, even though she really wanted to. She remembered that Gavin told her that she was not ready to marry him. "Did Gavin decide to marry me just to prove to Derrick that he was wrong?" She thought.

"I don't know what to say," said Dina.

"Just say yes," replied Gavin

"You told me that I was not ready to marry you." Said Dina

"It was more than three years ago, now I think that you are more than ready." Replied Gavin

"What makes you think that I'm ready now," asked Dina

"Many things, you put yourself back to graduate school and earned your law degree while earning a living, and taking care of your son," explained Gavin

Dina could not believe that Gavin knew about things that were happening in her life, even though they have not seen each other in about four years.

"How did you know about all of this?" asked Dina

"Because I was not far from you as you thought, but what truly showed me that you are really ready to be my wife is the fact that you just refused a marriage proposal from Derrick." Said Gavin

"Oh, you were listening?" Asked Dina, surprised.

"Yes, and Derrick saw me from the start," said Gavin

'That's why he kept on looking around,' realized Dina

"I'm still waiting for your answer. Dina, will you marry me?" asked Gavin

"I don't know, my life is so complicated now. You were right when you warned me about marrying Derrick just for revenge. I never stopped paying the price of it, how are we going to manage all of this?" replied Dina

"I don't know exactly how, but what I do know is that, whatever comes next, we will be ready to overcome it. We have been through so much and our love has survived. So, for the third time, Dina Joseph, will you marry me?" asked Gavin

"Yes, yes, yes" replied Dina

"Not so fast," Said Derrick who was silent until now, "*our son* is still waiting for us. We are supposed to celebrate your graduation as a family, not the other way around."

Gavin was about to answer Derrick, but Dina touched him by his arm, to let her reply instead.

"Fine Derrick, I tried to play it nice with you, but I don't think that you get it; so, listen, our son is a child, he cannot decide of whether or not you should join us. You are the adult, so I will tell you something without sugar coating it for you: stay the heck out of my house!" Said Dina

"Wow, you're really going to do that to Ethan? He needs both of us in his life," replied Derrick

"What Ethan really needs is two loving parents. We can both love him without being together. It's my turn to dump you Derrick. I will never get back with you, and dragging our son into it won't help you at all." Said Dina.

As Gavin was holding Dina's hand, a poem of love came to her mind:
"I have experienced both love and hate
Hate had caused me to be furious and angry
Love had made me calm and happy
So, I choose to love before it's too late"

I found them, they are over there, they are over there," yelled Ethan Joyfully.

Dina's parents walked towards her and were surprised to see Gavin. He was arm in arm with Dina, and Derrick was standing alone.

"Hi, Gavin" said Ethan

"Hey buddy, how are you?" Asked Gavin, while giving him a high-five

"Doctor Lawrence," said Dina's father, "it's been a long time, how are you?" He added

"Please, call me Gavin. I'm doing good thank you. I came to congratulate Dina on her achievements." Said Gavin

Dina's mother was looking at the ring on Dina's finger, and was overjoy,

Dina showed her hand with the ring, and announced the news to her parents:

"Gavin and I are getting married." Said Dina.

"Well, Gavin, welcome to the family!" Said Dina's father; her mother echoed it.

"Thank you, Mr. and Mrs. Joseph," I really appreciate it. I want you to know that I truly love your daughter, and I promise that I will respect and cherish her, and I will do everything in my power to protect her all the days of my life.

"I know you will," replied her father.

Dina was amazed by the amount of respect that Gavin was showing to her parents, and how willing he was to promise to value and respect her. She was also very excited to become his wife and was looking forward to all the memories that she was going to make with him. "I am definitely ready to marry Gavin, I love him" she thought. For once, they were on the same page, and the contentment that Dina was experiencing was astounding...

A poem of thanksgiving to God came to her mind:

"As we read in the Bible,
It is so admirable
All the Lord has done for us
That praying Him in Jesus
He fills our heart with peace and joy
Our pain He has destroy"

"I think it's time for us to go home," said Dina. "My mother has prepared a small reception; would you like to join us?"

"It will be my pleasure," replied Gavin.

"Is daddy coming with us?" asked Ethan.

"No, baby. Your father needs to take care of some business, but, soon, you will start graduating from school, and he will be able to participate at the celebrations with us, okay?" Said Dina.

"Okay," answered Ethan. "Can I say bye to him?" he asked

"Sure," answered Dina.

Ethan ran to Derrick and hugged his legs. His father gently massaged his head and kissed him. Ethan quickly returned to his mother.

Dina took Ethan's hand, and Gavin held his other hand. All three walked to the parking lot with Dina's parents. "I am so happy that this part of my life is over, I have learned the hard way how revenge is an awful act that can lead people to a self-destructive path. Thanks be to God that I finally found love." Thought Dina.

Derrick stood there looking at Dina and Gavin walking with Ethan. It was heart wrenching for him to see the two people that he loved the most in this world walking away without him. He never thought that one day, he would come back to Dina, and she would reject him. "If only I had not cheated on her again when she gave me that second chance..." Thought Derrick. He realized that you can only know what someone really meant to you when you push them away and cannot win them back...

*****

About the Author

Guerline Fenelon Jean Pierre was born and raised in Port-au-Prince, Haiti. She resides in Silver Spring, Maryland, and attended Montgomery College. She has been writting since she was sixteen and published her first book – a children book called Little Jebb and the Giant Fire Eyes – in 2014.

Visit her at: Facebook.com/@guerlinefjeanpierre

www.ingramcontent.com/pod-product-compliance
Lightning Source LLC
Chambersburg PA
CBHW030227180626
46810CB00008B/3010